ODDS ON MURDER

A Charley Hall Mystery, Book 4

Brenda Gayle

BOWSTRING
BOOKS

BOWSTRING
BOOKS

Odds on Murder
(A Charley Hall Mystery, Book 4)
by Brenda Gayle

Published Internationally by Bowstring Books
Ottawa, Ontario, Canada
Copyright © 2020 Brenda G Heald
Print Edition Copyright © 2021 Brenda G Heald

EBOOK ISBN 978-1-9990185-9-7
PRINT ISBN 978-1-7775824-4-9

For Bruce, Sean, Makenzie & Zack, my self-isolation buddies
during this unusual time.

Charley Hall could feel his warm breath on her neck. She kept her head down and concentrated on completing the paragraph she was typing on the portable, red Smith-Corona typewriter she carted back and forth to the office most days. The ability to focus was something she'd become very good at after six years of working in the noisy newsroom of the *Kingston Tribune*.

Why was he bothering her anyway? She was an hour away from deadline. If she ignored him, maybe he'd go away.

He cleared his throat.

Then again, when was the last time he'd approached her desk? He preferred to bellow at her from across the newsroom.

She stopped typing and slowly spun her chair to look up into the bespectacled eyes of John Sherman, the *Trib*'s managing editor. "Can I help you with something?" she said, her sweet voice dripping with sarcasm.

"Can you come to my office?" His voice was barely louder than a whisper.

"Now? I have to finish this piece on royal baby fashion."

"What's that?"

Charley sighed at the incredulity on his face. This was hardly the type of hard news she wanted to be writing, either, but a few days ago Princess Elizabeth gave birth to her first child, a son and future king, and—trivial or not—readers of the women's pages would expect *something* on the subject. "Never mind." She stood. "Let's go."

"Close the door," Sherman said, taking his seat behind his desk. He didn't bother asking her to sit down. She rarely did in his office. It was a power-play between them. A self-conscious, five-foot-four Sherman had his desk and chair raised on blocks so he could appear to look down on visitors seated across from him. Charley, at five-foot-seven, preferred to remain standing. It was difficult enough being the *Trib*'s sole female reporter; she'd take any advantage she could.

Patience didn't come easily to her, but she'd realized that exercised properly, it could be another advantage, so she waited while Sherman fiddled with a pile of papers on his desk, his eyes periodically darting up at her. Finally, he expelled a long breath and asked, "Have you seen Pyne recently?"

The question caught her totally off guard. Lester Pyne. Her nemesis. The bane of her existence. Okay, so that was a little over-dramatic, but the man had taken her job as city reporter, relegating her to the women's pages. "No," she said. And then before she could stop herself, "Why?"

Darn it! From the gleam in Sherman's eyes, he'd been hoping she'd ask. "He hasn't been in the office for a few days," he said.

"I hadn't noticed." Behind her back, her fingers crossed as a superstitious take-back of the lie. Of course, she'd noticed. She noticed everything Lester Pyne did and didn't do. She was waiting for him to screw up so she could prove to Sherman that the man wasn't up to the job —her job.

"I'd like you to go around and check on him."

"Me?" she squeaked.

"Yeah, you." He pushed the wire-rimmed glasses up onto his head and rubbed his eyes. "If it's something to do with the job, you might be able to help him."

"And if it's not?"

He shrugged. "It would be better coming from a woman. I mean, if he's dealing with...you know...?"

She waited.

"If it's something personal," he snapped. "You know, maybe something related to adjusting to being back from the war. You have experience with that."

Charley sank onto the couch. Yes, she had experience with that. Her brother, Freddie. Two-and-a-half years after VE day he still couldn't talk about what had happened to him over there; how could she expect a complete stranger to do so? And frankly, she didn't want him to.

"I don't know where he lives." She was too taken aback by the request to come up with anything better.

Sherman, of course, interpreted her feeble excuse as acquiescence. "Talk to Miss Fletcher. She can give you his home address, as well as what he was working on." He lowered his glasses and opened a file on his desk. She was dismissed.

Miss Fletcher.

Grace.

The *Tribune*'s archivist was the one person John Sherman showed any real deference to. Probably because he knew the place would collapse without her. With a degree in library science, she'd joined the staff not long after Charley to manage the mountain of information the reporters generated and to catalogue articles from all the *Trib*'s published editions. However, she'd quickly proven to be a top-notch researcher, too. Grace could ferret out those seemingly innocuous details that would break a story wide open.

And she was the only other woman working for the newspaper.

Charley pushed open the door to the archives—known as the morgue—and called out to her friend.

"Oh good." Grace tucked a wayward strand of her long, blonde hair behind her ear. "I found some old baby photographs of Princess Elizabeth and her sister, Margaret, which I thought you could use with your article. Here, let me show you." She slipped off her stool and walked over to a long counter where she'd arranged a series of images.

Charley scanned them briefly. "Thanks, these are great. But they're not why I'm here."

Grace leaned back against the counter and cocked her head, her pale blue eyes concerned. "Is something wrong? Is it Freddie?"

She shook her head. "No, Freddie seems to be doing better since Laine was moved up to the fourth floor."

Grace looked away and tried to surreptitiously wipe at a tear. Dr. Laine Black, Grace's dear friend and roommate, had been grievously injured a few months earlier and had spent several weeks in a coma, kept alive by a mechanical respirator. She was making slow progress toward recovery due to a serious head injury, and no one could say whether or not she would ever return to the intelligent, vivacious woman she'd been before. A few weeks previous, she'd been moved from intensive care on the second floor up to the fourth floor, which housed the shell-shocked soldiers who'd returned from the war—many of whom had once been her patients.

"He's been reading to her, you know," Grace said.

That was news to Charley. Thanks to Grace and Laine —and a sailboat christened as the *Lady Stonebridge*—her brother had finally seemed to be overcoming his alcohol addiction until the attack on Laine had sent him back to the bottle. "I had no idea. I did know he had started that new sobriety program that's been in the news."

"Yes. And he's resumed his studies at Queen's University." Grace peered at Charley. "You didn't know?"

"I haven't spoken to him very much these past few months." Charley didn't add that Freddie was deliberately avoiding her and Gran—and well he should after the stunt he'd pulled after Labour Day.

"Well, if it's not Freddie and it's not Laine, why are you looking so glum?"

"Lester Pyne."

Grace's eyes widened in surprise and she turned away to stack and straighten the princesses' baby photographs.

"Grace?"

The archivist picked up a pencil and turned back to Charley, her face a mask of indifference. "What about him?" Her voice was too casual.

Charley eyed her friend. "John Sherman asked me to check on him."

"He asked *you*? Why would he do that?"

"I don't know. Because he hasn't been in the newsroom for a few days, and I guess Sherman's worried. Now you're making me think there might be something to it."

Grace hesitated, tapping the pencil against her thigh.

Charley was certain something was going on. Grace was never this secretive—not with her, and not about Lester

Pyne, whom they both agreed shouldn't have stolen Charley's job. "C'mon, Grace, what gives?"

Grace turned to the counter and scribbled onto a notepad. Then she tore off the sheet and handed it to Charley. "This is his home address."

"I was going to telephone him," Charley said.

She shook her head. "Better to go see him. I wouldn't trust the telephone."

"Do you know what he was working on?"

Grace nodded and handed her a manila-coloured enve-lope. Charley opened it and withdrew a single typewritten page. She recognized it immediately.

She scanned the document, but there was no more information now than there had been when Grace had shown it to her several months ago. "Colin Banks?"

"Lester came to me a month ago and asked me to see what I could find out about him. I gave him what I had dug up for you. He thinks it's odd, too, that there is nothing about him before he arrived in Kingston two years ago."

Charley's reporter instincts wondered if she'd let a scoop get away—lost an opportunity to get her old job back. But Grace hadn't given her the information for a story. It had been personal. And it wasn't Colin Banks she'd been interested in, anyway; it was his sister, Meredith—the woman whose engagement to her childhood friend, Alderman Dan Cannon, had both stunned and devastated her. She'd barely spoken to Dan since the announcement.

"Has he found anything?" Charley asked.

Grace shrugged. "All I know is that it's Wednesday and no one has heard from him since he left here Friday night."

Now it was making sense. "You alerted Sherman."

Grace nodded. "He doesn't keep close tabs on his reporters' comings and goings, as you well know. All he

6

cares about is getting a scoop. I'm sorry, Charley. I didn't think you'd be the one he'd ask to check up on Lester. But I'm worried. He's still a fairly new reporter. What if he's gotten in over his head...or something worse has happened to him?"

"Mrs. Hall?"

Charley raised her gaze to meet Romeo Arcadi's questioning eyes in the rear-view mirror of the taxi.

We're here already?

The address Grace had given her was northeast of the *Trib*'s offices. She'd contemplated walking, but the afternoon was chilly and overcast and, given it was mid-November, the sun was setting earlier and earlier. By four-thirty it would be dusk.

"I don't mind sitting here for a bit if you need some time," Arcadi said.

"What about your paying customers?" she asked. He absolutely refused to accept any money from her and yet, every time she called to request a cab, it was Arcadi who arrived.

He shrugged. "They can wait."

"I should get this over with." Before she even had time to collect her hat and satchel, Arcadi had donned his poor boy cap, rounded the cab and opened her door. "Don't wait for me," she admonished him, accepting his hand for assistance.

"No ma'am but do call when you're ready to leave."

Charley hesitated on the sidewalk. Lester's home was in

one of the neighbourhoods that had sprung up in the early 1940s as temporary housing for workers in the local aluminum factory. The cookie-cutter, one-and-a-half storey houses all had the same clapboard walls and small sash windows. Inside, she knew there'd be a living room, kitchen with a dining area, bathroom and one bedroom on the main floor. Two additional bedrooms were tucked upstairs under the steeply pitched roof.

Before her demotion to the women's pages, she'd done a story on how Kingston was adapting and expanding the Kingscourt Neighbourhood model to other parts of the city to provide housing for returning soldiers and their families.

Who was it she'd interviewed about it at City Hall? Palmer something, wasn't it? What did it matter? She was stalling. The cab ride hadn't been nearly long enough to figure out what she was going to say to Lester.

Hello, Lester, I just happened to be in the neighbourhood and thought I'd pop by...

Hi, Lester, John Sherman says you haven't been around the office lately and asked me to check up on you...

Hey, Lester, I hear you're looking into Colin Banks...

She should accept the inevitable. There was no way this wasn't going to be awkward for both of them.

Darn you, John Sherman.

"Are you lost?"

Charley jumped. She hadn't noticed the young woman coming toward her. "No, thank you. "She pointed at the house she'd stopped in front of. "516. That's what I'm looking for."

"Oh? That's my home."

Charley looked closer at the woman. She was wearing a man's grey woolen coat, which seemed too large for her. Her hair was loose, allowing the long dark curls to cascade down from beneath the blue knit cap. Her head was cocked to the side, but the expression in her warm hazel eyes was one of curiosity, not concern. She shifted the bag she was carrying to her other hand and adjusted the pocketbook that had been about to slip out from where she'd pinned it under her arm.

"I'm here to see Lester Pyne," Charley said. "I was told he lives here."

The woman's face brightened. "I know who you are," she said, grinning. "You're Charley Hall, from the *Tribune*, aren't you?"

"Yes, I am."

"I knew it! Les has told me all about you." Her voice was breathless. "I'm Eleanor, his wife. Come in, please."

Told me all about you?

She and Lester had barely had more than a half-dozen conversations since he joined the *Trib* six months ago, and all of them had been related to the job. Charley knew nothing about him except he'd fought in the war. Heck, she hadn't even known he was married.

"Les," Eleanor called as they entered the home. She put down the bag and, in her haste to unbutton her coat, she dropped the pocketbook. "Les! We have a guest."

"Shhhh!" Lester scolded as he emerged from a back room, gently bouncing a blue-blanketed bundle on his shoulder. "I finally got him to sleep."

A baby, too?

He stopped when he saw Charley, his expression as flustered as her own must have appeared. "Mrs. Hall?"

Eleanor picked up her bag and pocketbook. "Don't stand there, Lester. Invite her to have a seat. I'll make a pot of tea." She went to her husband as if she meant to relieve him of the baby, but realizing her hands were full, she shook her head, bemused. "I'll take him after I've put on the kettle."

Charley glanced around the living room and selected a straight-back, upholstered chair across from the sofa. Lester took the other single chair in the room—a brown leather smoking chair that had seen better days.

It was odd seeing Lester away from the *Trib*. Rather than his usual ill-fitting suit, he was wearing a long-sleeved flannel shirt and belted navy trousers. Slightly balding and with that mama's boy look, Lester had a doughiness to him that always made it difficult for her to imagine him as a soldier fighting in Europe. It was almost as hard to imagine him with a wife and a child.

"What's his name?" Charley asked to break the uncomfortable silence.

"Anthony. After Eleanor's father." Lester glanced down at his son, a look of rapture on his face.

"How old?"

"Five months tomorrow."

A young woman—a girl, really—danced into the room. "Ellie asked me to take the babe," she said, lifting Anthony off Lester's shoulder.

He seemed reluctant to let him go and his gaze followed them as they left the room.

"Your nanny?" Charley asked.

Lester turned back, his eyebrows raised in surprise, and then he gave her a mocking grin and chuckled darkly. "My wife's brother's girlfriend," he said. "Linda. She and Emerson live with us to help with costs."

Charley closed her eyes and wished she could disappear.

A nanny? Really, Charley!

Wasn't this just the type of social elitism Mark always accused her of.

Darn it, and darn Mark Spadina!

Even though she'd cut off all contact with him—told him she never wanted to see him again—the private detective had a habit of slipping into her thoughts. Usually when she messed up, like now. "I'm sorry, I—"

Lester held up his hands to stop her from continuing. "Look, Mrs. Hall, I know you don't like me very much, and I can't say as I blame you. But I need this job. I have a family to provide for. It's not a hobby to me."

"It's not a hobby to me, either!"

"Fair enough. But I dare say, if you were to lose it, you wouldn't be destitute, out on the streets begging for whatever scraps you can find."

"I—"

"You may think I'm exaggerating, but I assure you, I am not. I know a number of blokes who survived everything Jerry could throw at them only to come back home and lose all they thought they'd been fighting for." He reached into his breast pocket and took out a cigarette. He placed it between his lips and dug into the pocket of his trousers, searching for something to light it with.

"Lester Pyne!" Eleanor reprimanded him as she carried a tray into the room.

"Sorry," he said, and sheepishly plucked the cigarette out of his mouth and tucked it behind his ear.

"I've asked him to stop smoking in the house," Eleanor said, placing the tray on a low table across from the sofa. "For the baby."

A lanky young man with unkempt dark hair stalked into the room and slumped down on the couch beside Eleanor. She introduced Charley to her brother, Emerson, and smiled appreciatively at Charley when she insisted everyone use her given name rather than "Mrs. Hall."

"Is Linda going to join us?" Eleanor asked her brother.

"Nah, she's staying with the babe." He reached out and took a cookie, earning a look of rebuke from his sister.

"Perhaps you can pass the plate around, Em?" she said.

Charley took one of the cookies—oatmeal raisin, her favourite—and thanked the surly young man.

"I've been a big fan of yours for such a long time, Charley," Eleanor said as she poured out four cups of tea. "I was absolutely beside myself when Les said he'd gotten a job at the *Tribune*." She nudged Emerson, who reluctantly rose to hand Charley and Lester their cups. "You could have knocked me over with a feather when he told me the great Charley Hall was a woman!"

Charley felt the heat from the blush creeping up her face. "Sherman thought it would be better if we didn't publicize that given the type of stories I was working on."

"Of course. I remember that wonderful *exposé* you did on Alderman Delaney." She shifted her gaze to Lester. "It was while you were in England. The Alderman was siphoning off money meant to run his ward office so he could pay for a flat for his mistress." She giggled. "Oh, it was quite the scandal."

Charley grinned. She'd spent months tracking the activities of Timothy Delaney. In the end, his mistress had turned on him because he'd refused to leave his wife as he'd promised her. Both the mistress and wife had given Charley exclusive interviews, and Delaney had spent several months in jail. While neither woman would take him back, his constituents had been more forgiving and re-elected him the following year. "He is remarrying, you know," Charley said. "The announcement will appear in this weekend's *Trib*."

"How wonderful. I can't wait to find out what she's like." Eleanor glanced toward her husband. "Lester doesn't cotton to that style of reporting, do you, dear?"

Lester took a sip of his tea but didn't respond.

No, Charley thought, he doesn't cotton to it at all. Lester's reporting was dry and dull, just the facts. There was no colour, no human interest. If he'd been a better reporter, she might not be quite so bitter about him replacing her.

"Are the two of you working on a story together?" Eleanor sounded excited. "Is that why you're here?"

"Yes, Mrs.—ah, Charley—why are you here?" Lester asked.

Charley washed down the last of the cookie she'd eaten with a sip of tea. Both were delicious. Gran would approve. "You haven't been at the *Trib* for the past few—"

"Oh, that's my fault," Eleanor interrupted. "The baby's had a cough and it's kept me up at night. Lester has been staying home so I can rest during the day. Today is the first day I've had any energy at all."

"And he sent you out shopping?" Charley couldn't help herself.

"Oh, no." Eleanor giggled and grinned at her husband. "I've been desperate for weeks to get out on my own—all by myself—for a few hours. Les, such a dear, said that since I was feeling stronger today and he was at home, I should go out and buy myself something." Her eyes shone. "Which I did!"

A crimson flush extended from Lester's neck up to the top of his balding head but, given the way he was looking at his wife, Charley could see he adored Eleanor. She felt a tug of longing. What would it be like to have someone look at her that way? "That's lovely," she said.

"I can't tell you what it is." Eleanor winked. "Oh, I'll tell you, Les, of course I will. I'll even show you...later."

"Oh, brother." Emerson groaned. He stood and left without acknowledging anyone in the room, and without even thanking his sister for the tea and cookies.

Such rudeness.

Gran would have sent them to bed without supper if she or Freddie had behaved that way in front of guests—even if no guests had been present.

"Grace tells me you're looking into Colin Banks," Charley said, and then glanced anxiously at Eleanor.

"It's all right. I don't keep anything from Ellie," Lester said. "Yes, Colin Banks is a mystery. Your friend Alderman Cannon is engaged to his sister, correct? Have you met him?"

Charley shook her head. "I've met Meredith, his sister, but not Colin—at least we've not been formally introduced. I did hear him speak at the engagement party." She remembered a short, round man who gave the impression of someone older than his thirty or so years. "He has an accent, which I can't place."

"South African," Lester said. "I heard him speak at a city council meeting and recognized it right away. I knew some chaps from Johannesburg who flew with the RAF."

"You flew with the Royal Air Force?" she asked, immediately regretting the incredulity in her voice.

A familiar expression appeared on Lester's face. She'd seen it on many of the men who returned from war and would rather talk about anything other than their experiences.

"Yes and no," he replied cryptically. Then he heaved a sigh. "I was a quartermaster in England for the RAF. And no, I never saw battle. Flat feet."

"But it was a very important job," Eleanor said. "They couldn't have flown without you."

The quartermaster was responsible for procuring all of the military's material goods from clothing to weapons, and everything in between. He was required to understand and anticipate the needs of the troops and have the ingenuity to develop reliable supply chains—as well as the flexibility to improvise when they failed. As Eleanor said, it was an important job, and one not given to any old recruit who had flat feet.

"There are a lot of ways to fight a war that don't involve going into battle," Charley said, reluctantly acknowledging the growing respect she was beginning to feel toward Lester.

"Right." He started to take a sip from his cup but realizing it was empty, put it down. "About Colin Banks. I could use your help if you're willing. But I need to warn you, I think this could lead down some shady back alleys."

"You think he's crooked? Do you think Dan's involved?" She may not share the same close relationship with her friend as they'd once had, but she wasn't about to be involved in an attempt to smear him. Quite the opposite. She'd protected him in the past and she was quite certain she'd do so again.

"Nah, not him. At least I haven't come across anything to suggest it. But there are things going on at City Hall that don't pass the smell test. I haven't had much luck on my own, but you've got connections there that I don't. If you're willing to use them, I think we can get to the bottom of it."

Charley leaned back in her chair and stared into her teacup. Then she raised her gaze and uttered a sentence she never thought she'd hear herself say: "Okay, Lester, you've got yourself a partner."

THE SUN HAD ALREADY SET by the time Charley climbed the steps to her family's red brick colonial home on King Street West. She dropped her satchel in the foyer and placed her pocketbook on the table.

Rachel, her grandmother's latest housekeeper, hurried toward her, helping to remove her coat and taking her hat and gloves. "Mrs. Stormont has already eaten and is now retiring in the drawing room," she said, hanging the garments on the coat tree. "I am to bring you a dinner tray in there."

Charley thanked her and made her way to the drawing room.

"Good evening, Gran. I'm sorry I'm so late." Charley bent down to kiss her grandmother's soft weathered cheek before settling into her favourite chair, a moss-coloured *bergère* armchair.

Elizabeth—Bessie—Stormont's lips compressed to a thin line of disapproval. "You know I don't like to eat alone." She closed the book she'd been reading and set it on the side table.

"Where's Freddie?"

"Who knows these days?"

Charley bit back an irritated rejoinder. Her brother,

unreliable since his return from the war, had become a ghost in their home over the past few months, appearing for the occasional meal while revealing nothing about his comings and goings. Grace's remark that he'd been reading to Laine had been the first solid information she'd received about what he'd been up to. "I am sorry, Gran, but it couldn't be helped. Mr. Sherman insisted I check on a co-worker who hasn't been in the office for several days."

Rachel glided into the room and placed the tray on the sideboard, her dark hair perfectly pinned back, and her uniform impeccably pressed despite a full day of service. Charley watched as she removed the cover from the plate, poured a glass of water and arranged the cutlery just so before placing the tray on Charley's lap. Of all her grand-mother's housekeepers, Rachel Winters was one of the best they'd ever had—at least since she and her brother had come to live with her grandparents twenty-five years ago. Despite her relatively young age—Charley estimated it to be around twenty-nine, like her—the woman possessed a proficiency that many in her profession took years to master. She was the perfect housekeeper and Charley didn't like her one bit.

"I don't know why you keep her on," Charley said when Rachel had left the room.

"She is a very good housekeeper."

"I don't trust her."

"Well, trust is a whole other matter. I trust her not to steal the silver." Bessie grinned.

"That's not what I'm talking about, and you know it."

Bessie's expression sobered. "Yes, I know what you're talking about."

"She had to have known Evelyn—or of her, at least. How?"

"Perhaps she merely researched our family before

coming to work here. That may be something a good domestic would do. It's certainly not a crime."

Charley eyed Gran skeptically. "Have you ever known a housekeeper to take that much interest in a family? Up until two months ago, we'd had no contact with Lady Evelyn Pierrepont for decades, and certainly none could have been anticipated. There would be absolutely no reason for Rachel to have even known about her, let alone to address her by her hereditary title of Thorton." Charley had lost her appetite and put the tray on the table beside her. Every time she thought about the sudden arrival of her maternal grandmother from England she felt ill.

"I keep her on because she is an exceptionally good, reliable housekeeper and, as you well know, those are hard to find. But I also want to see what happens when Evelyn returns from her cross-country sojourn. If, indeed, there is some connection between her and Rachel, I am curious to learn what that is."

"I think she's a spy," Charley said.

Bessie nodded her head. "It's possible. But if so, don't you want to find out what information it is that Evelyn is so desperate to get her hands on?"

"She's desperate to get her hands on Freddie, that's for certain."

"Hi-dee-ho." A male voice called from the hallway.

"Speak of the devil," Charley murmured and then called out, "We're in the drawing room," earning a look of rebuke from Gran for yelling from one room to another.

Freddie sauntered in, gave both Bessie and Charley perfunctory kisses on their cheeks and then sunk onto the sofa. "Are you going to eat that?" He motioned to Charley's tray. "I told Rachel not to bother making me a plate, but it smells so good it's making me hungry."

"Help yourself," Charley said.

Her brother looked better than she'd seen him in a long time. His red beard was neatly trimmed, and his hair had been barbered recently, too. But it was his serene expression that made her catch her breath. Ever since he'd returned from the war, he'd been tormented by what he'd seen, done, and had done to him, while fighting the Nazis. He'd looked for solace in a bottle rather than confide in anyone. Several times, he'd tried to get sober, and each time something would break him. The Freddie sitting across from her now, devouring the chicken pot pie, reminded her of the innocent young man who'd joined the army in '39 seeking adventure and the opportunity to serve his country.

When he finished, Freddie put down his fork and dabbed his mustache with the napkin. "That was delicious."

"I'm glad you enjoyed it," Bessie said dryly. "Perhaps you'd care to attend a meal or two at the appointed hour."

"I'll try," Freddie said, giving her a dazzling smile. He turned and winked conspiratorially at Charley as if their tendency to arrive home after dinner was some sort of sibling club they belonged to. He stood. "I'll take this back to the kitchen and give Rachel my thanks."

"You just got here, do you have to leave?" Charley asked. "I thought we could catch up. We've barely spoken in weeks."

"I'd love to, but it will have to wait. I have an essay due on Shakespeare's Sonnet 29 tomorrow. 'When in disgrace with fortune and men's eyes,' and all that." He paused on the threshold. "Oh, and don't forget, Grandmama is returning this weekend."

Great!

"If you're not careful, that scowl will become permanent," Bessie teased Charley when they were alone again.

"I don't want her here," Charley said. Evelyn had spent a week with them when she arrived in September, but for the last two months she'd been travelling by train across the country to admire the fall foliage and then visiting friends in Toronto.

"I'm not overjoyed at the thought of her being with us until spring, either," Bessie said, "But your brother invited her."

"That's the other thing I don't understand. The war ended in '45, but it took a year for him to return to Kingston. All he'll tell us is that he was in a German POW camp. But he's never said where he was after the camps were liberated. Then *she* shows up two years later, and lets it slip that he'd been in England with her."

"And that he is the heir to the Earldom of Thorton," Bessie added. "Has he said anything more to you about that? Is he planning to return to the Midlands with her in the spring?"

"He hasn't said anything about anything. He never does." Charley had been reluctant to press for details given Freddie's fragile mental state, but the more time that passed, the harder it was to accept his silence. She needed answers. What had happened at Dieppe? Why had he been declared missing, presumed dead? Why had he delayed his return home after the war ended?

And, of course, where was her husband, Theo?

CHARLEY WATCHED Grace prepare the three cups of tea. She knew it was ridiculous to be annoyed that her friend was as familiar with how Lester took his—four scoops of sugar, no milk—as she was with how Charley liked hers —clear.

She accepted her cup with thanks and turned back to Lester. His last statement had landed with a thud into their conversation. "Murdered? Are you certain?"

"Of course not. It's speculation at this point. But look at the evidence." Lester's surly expression softened as he accepted his tea from Grace and took a grateful sip.

"The official report said it was an accident, that Alderman Smythe fell off his roof while doing some repairs."

It had been months ago. Early summer. Charley remembered reading about it, but it hadn't been her story—Lester had already replaced her on the city beat by then.

"Do you know what Smythe did for a living—aside from serving as alderman?" Lester didn't wait for her to reply. "Roofer."

That got her attention. "The police didn't think that was suspicious?"

Lester shook his head. "Nah, no witnesses and nothing to prove foul play. It was ruled an accident."

"But you don't believe it."

"He's up on roofs day in and day out for years. You mean to tell me that he slips and falls fixing his own—on a clear, sunny day? It smells like rotten fish to me."

She agreed it was strange, but strange things happened all the time. A roofer falling off a roof wasn't impossible—improbable, maybe, but it could be a matter of odds. Charley turned to Grace. "What do you think?"

"I think you need to hear the rest."

"As you probably know, Kingston's city council is planning to annex parts of Kingston Township. This would expand the city's western municipal boundary, and Alderman Smythe's ward, to the mouth of the Little Cataraqui River, on the north shore of Lake Ontario," Lester said. "Last spring, a group of investors announced plans to buy up land even further west—out to Gardiners Road—to develop it for homes and businesses. But to be profitable, they need the city to change its land-use plans and include that area in the next annexation, too. Smythe was against it. He felt it was too much too soon, and worried that such a large land-grab—his words—would adversely affect his constituents."

"Gardiners Road? That's the middle of nowhere. There's nothing out there but a bunch of farms," Charley said. "It will take years for the city to reach out that far."

"Not that many years at the rate we're growing," Lester said. "There's a drive-in theatre that's already opened out there, and I've been told a hotel is part of the proposal, too."

"So, with Alderman Smythe out of the way—"

"And the very pro-development Arthur Carruthers elected to replace him—" Lester interjected.

"—there will be no serious opposition at council to stop the investors' push to increase the area of annexation." Charley took a moment to let the information sink in. "And let me guess, Colin Banks is one of those investors."

"Yessiree. He's listed as the primary investor," Lester said.

Charley turned to Grace. "You've found nothing more on him?"

Grace's expression darkened. "It's as if he suddenly materialized from thin air—along with a great sum of money."

Charley nodded. She'd been to his enormous limestone mansion on Front Road and knew he'd bought up many properties in the downtown's business section. "But he's done nothing illegal, so far as we know," Charley said.

"Nothing I can find."

"Most of the property he currently owns is in your pal Alderman Cannon's ward," Lester said. "Plus, Cannon's engaged to his sister. I was thinking you could see if he knows more about the family and where their money came from."

Charley also knew that Colin Banks was slated to be Dan's campaign manager once he announced his intention to run for federal office, but no one in the room was aware of that. Dan was as honest a politician as she had ever known —and it wasn't their long friendship that made her feel that way. She was certain he'd never associate himself with someone whose past was questionable—not when his political future was at stake.

"Look, Hall, I'm not saying that Cannon is implicated in any of this. And I'm not even saying that Banks is crooked. I'd like to know more before I publish anything," Lester said.

"He's right," Grace said. "Just because I can't find anything, doesn't mean there's anything shady about Banks' past." She cocked her head and grinned at Charley. "Well, except that business about his wife being a murderer and trying to kill you, of course."

"There is that." Charley shuttered at the memory of her close call with death. "But he married Adeline after he moved to Kingston and established himself."

"Canada has taken in a lot of displaced wealthy Europeans since the war ended. In many cases, records have been lost or destroyed." Grace shrugged helplessly.

"But Banks isn't European," Charley said. "He's South African. Isn't that what you said?" She looked to Lester who nodded.

"You didn't tell me that." Grace glared at Lester.

"I didn't think it was important."

"Well, of course it's important," Grace snapped. "I've been looking in the wrong hemisphere." Belying the crossness of her tone, Grace's face lit up with excitement. She slid off her stool, collected the teacups, and shooed Charley and Lester from the morgue.

"So, what's next?" Charley asked as she followed Lester through the newsroom's labyrinth of desks. She felt as invigorated as Grace: the anticipation, the pursuit, the conquest. Finding a story and chasing it to its conclusion—this was what she lived for. Her talent was wasted on the women's pages.

"You talk to Cannon. See if he knows anything—even if you could get a sense of his take on Carruthers, that would be helpful." Lester reached into his breast pocket and withdrew a half-empty package of Chesterfield cigarettes. He tapped one of the stubby white cylinders into his hand, replaced the pack, and fished for a lighter. "I'm going to get in touch with my contact at City Hall and see if I can get a look-see at that hotel proposal."

CHARLEY TIGHTENED the scarf around her neck to fend off the chilly air. She'd decided the hour-long walk to City Hall would be the best way to blow off the stench of cigarette smoke that always hovered like a cloud over the *Tribune*'s newsroom. She'd never been fond of the pungent herbaceous smell, but since Lester Pyne's arrival, it seemed more odious. She didn't know if it was the brand he smoked or the quantity.

The sweet and spicy aroma of pipe tobacco, on the other hand, brought back wonderful memories of sitting on her grandfather's lap while he read to her from that day's edition of the *Tribune,* the broadsheet he founded and continued to publish until he sold it in the mid-1930s. She'd seen a few photographs of her father with a pipe, too, usually from his time as a war correspondent but also relaxing with her mother on their sailboat, the *Lady Stonebridge*. Freddie had never taken up the habit, but that didn't surprise her. Her brother seemed to go out of his way to reject anything that would tie him to a Stormont legacy.

She paused on the corner of Ontario and Brock streets to secure her hat. It was breezier closer to the lake.

Maybe she should take up the vice. Some women did.

She remembered seeing an old entertainment magazine with actress Lupe Vélez smoking a pipe on the cover. Then again, the "Mexican Spitfire" had committed suicide a few years later, so perhaps she wasn't the best role model. Besides, Charley was quite certain Gran would have kittens if her granddaughter adopted yet another "male" affectation. She was already beside herself with Charley's penchant for wearing trousers rather than the much less practical skirt—and don't get her started about her nickname. Gran insisted on calling her "Charlotte" instead of "Charley."

Approaching the neo-classically designed City Hall building, she glanced up to one of the enormous clock faces that looked out from the cupola.

Ten-forty.

Darn it.

In the cold, she must have set a brisker pace than normal. Her appointment with Dan wasn't for another twenty minutes.

The fact she felt she needed to make an appointment with him didn't sit comfortably with her. And it hadn't escaped comment from his assistant, Diana Huff, either. In the past, Charley would waltz into Dan's office—either at City Hall or his family's shipyard—as it suited her. And, much to Diana's displeasure, she could always count on him to drop whatever he was doing to welcome her. But that was before...

She continued past the front entrance, rounded onto Market Street, and proceeded to the back of the building where the police station was housed.

"Well hello, Mrs. Hall, to what do we owe the pleasure?" Sergeant Jerry Kearn smiled at her from behind the counter and waved for her to come forward.

Charley smiled apologetically at the two other people who seemed to be lined up in front of her as she accepted Jerry's offer to jump the queue. She'd developed a good rapport with the sergeant, in no small part due to the cinnamon cakes she often brought with her—not as a bribe, mind you, but as a token of appreciation. Given his look of anticipation, she realized too late that she'd completely forgotten to stop at the market stall on her way in.

"I want to ask about an older case," she said, hoping Jerry wouldn't be too disappointed. "Alderman Smythe."

"Yeah, I remember. Fell off his roof. It was all over the news. What do you want to know?"

"Was there an investigation? A report that I can see?"

Jerry rocked back on his heels and gazed down at her. She suspected there must be a raised perch behind the counter to make the officers appear more authoritative—or menacing if the situation required—because she knew Jerry certainly wasn't tall enough to be looking down his nose at her from that height.

Must remember cinnamon cakes next time.

"Your pals Marillo and Adams were on that one. And today's your lucky day. They just brought someone in, so they're here. Go wait in the office and I'll send them to you when they've got the bloke settled in the cells."

Charley thanked him and crossed the lobby to the Sergeant's Office. She placed her hat and pocketbook on the desk, loosened her scarf and unbuttoned her coat. She glanced down to see if Jerry had unintentionally left any files on the desk. She should have known better. He never did.

"Mrs. Hall?" Constable Marillo stepped into the room followed by his partner, Constable Adams. "What can we help you with today?"

Charley's eyes darted between the two men. Marillo she quite liked, Adams, not so much. The younger officer had an air of superiority about him that she felt was unwarranted. He'd asked her out several times when he first joined the department, and her refusals seemed to have offended his male pride. He'd been curt and condescending toward her ever since.

She couldn't understand why Marillo, twenty years older, was still a constable. He gave off a quiet confidence that she found reassuring, even when she knew he was keeping things from her as he often tried to do.

"Why don't you go clean the cruiser before it stinks to high heaven," Marillo said to his partner.

Perceptive, too.

Adams threw Charley a nasty look and snorted indignantly. "Okay, but can you spot me a quarter so I can get a pack of smokes first?"

"Jeez, we got paid this week," Marillo said, but dug into his pocket and handed him the coin anyway. After Adams left, he grinned at Charley. "Brought a fellow in for drunk and disorderly, and he went and upchucked all over the backseat of the cruiser. I guess a quarter is a fair price for making him clean it up."

"Why are you always giving him money?" Charley asked. "It's not as if he's married with a family to support. Shouldn't he be able to buy his own smokes?"

"You would think so, wouldn't you, Mrs. Hall. Yes, you would definitely think so." He shrugged. "Now, what can I do for you?"

"Alderman Smythe. What can you tell me about his death?"

Marillo turned and walked toward the desk. He moved

34

Charley's hat and pocketbook out of the way and sat on the corner.

Stalling?

"It was an accident. He fell while he was up fixing his roof." His eyes narrowed. "What interest is this to the readers of the women's pages?"

"It's not. I'm helping another reporter on a story. I heard you investigated his death?"

"Uh-huh. But it was months ago. Why the interest now?"

"It may be related to something else. Did you notice anything inconsistent or unusual?"

"Actually, I wasn't there. Adams took the call and made the report."

"Where were you?"

"My dear Mrs. Hall," Marillo heaved a sigh of exasperation, "I realize you and everyone else in Kingston believe that police officers are at the beck and call of the citizens of this city, but I also have to answer to an even higher authority—my wife. She gets quite miffed with me if I don't take the occasional day off."

"Can I see the report?" she asked.

"No. He took a dive off his roof. Hit his head on the concrete below. Died on impact. End of story." Marillo stood. "If that's all..."

"Not quite. What do you know about Colin Banks? Has he had any involvement with the police?"

Marillo looked down to examine his scuffed, black leather boots.

Hesitating?

She waited.

"You mean aside from that trouble with his wife a few months back? No," he said, finally. "Now, if you'll excuse

me, I should go give Adams a hand cleaning up the puke."
He brushed past her.

"Would you tell me if there was?" Charley called
after him.

"No comment."

6

"Honestly, Charley, if you're going to go to all the trouble of making an appointment, it would be good if you actually arrived on time for it."

Charley flushed at Diana Huff's reprimand. Her meeting with Marillo had taken longer than planned and she was ten minutes late arriving at Dan's office.

There had never been any love lost between the two women. She was quite sure Diana harboured a secret crush on her boss and resented Charley's close friendship with Dan. Now that he was off the market, wouldn't it be funny if they became chums who bonded over their affection for the man who'd spurned them both?

Diana's eyebrows arched imperiously.

Nah, we'll never be friends.

Before Charley had an opportunity to form any sort of sarcastic reply, the door to Dan's office opened and he emerged with another man whom she recognized as Raymond Palmer. How coincidental. She'd been thinking about him only yesterday.

"Oh, Charley, I am so sorry. I'm running late. Have you been waiting long?" Dan asked as soon as he spotted her.

"Not too long," she said sliding a saccharine smile at

Diana before returning her attention to the two men. "Hello, Mr. Palmer, it's nice to see you again."

Palmer nodded his silver head in greeting. "Mrs. Hall." He turned and shook Dan's hand. "Thank you for your time, Alderman. I'll keep you updated."

"What was Raymond Palmer doing here?" Charley asked as she followed Dan into his office.

She tried not to be offended when he motioned for her to take a seat in one of the two straight-back chairs while he went to sit behind his desk. *So formal.* Usually, they sat together on the couch—but that was before everything changed between them.

"He works for the planning department," Dan said. "He was updating me on some projects that are coming before the council."

"Like the west-end development proposal?"

His eyes narrowed briefly and then his face relaxed, and she felt her heart give a jolt of recognition. It had been almost two months since she'd last seen him. He'd called several times, but she'd put him off. Now, sitting across from him, her mind and body remembered what it was like to be in his company.

It wasn't solely his movie-star looks with his sandy brown hair, whiskey-coloured eyes, strong chin, and athletic physique that made women swoon; it was the way he could make you feel as if there was no other person in the world who mattered more to him. She'd known him all her life and figured she'd been in love with him for about as long. And yet, when he'd asked her time and again to marry him, she'd refused.

Mark said it was because she knew Dan was the wrong man for her.

Stop it! It didn't matter what Mark Spadina said. He

was wrong. She couldn't marry Dan because she was still married to Theo.

She understood why he'd proposed to Meredith Banks. Understood that he needed a wife if he was going to run in the next federal election. But understanding didn't lessen the pain of knowing they would never again be as close as they'd once been.

"Don't get me wrong, I'm glad to see you, Charley— finally. But why are you here? Is it for me? Or are you here for a story?"

"Can't it be both?"

He chuckled and her heart flip-flopped again. She definitely needed to get her emotions under control.

"I wouldn't expect anything less." He threaded his fingers behind his head and leaned back in his chair. "Okay, shoot."

"What are your feelings about the new alderman, Arthur Carruthers?"

"Are we on the record?"

"Does it matter?"

"No, not really. I just like to know where reporter Charley stops and friend Charley begins."

Her heart broke a little bit more. "I will always be your friend, Dan."

The smile he returned was bittersweet. "I know." He sat up abruptly. "Okay, my take on Art Carruthers is that he's a politician's politician. He's got an agenda with the Township land west of the city and he's prepared to lobby for its annexation."

"Is that why Raymond Palmer was here?"

"No, that was something else entirely. And don't ask me because I can't talk about it."

She tucked away that piece of information. She

wouldn't push him on it now, but she'd let Lester know there might be something happening in Dan's ward he needed to keep an eye on. "Alderman Smythe had been against increasing the annexation, right?"

"Yeah, but after his death, his constituents voted for Carruthers, so it's possible Smythe was out of touch with his community's wishes. He'd been their alderman for a long time. It happens."

"Did you know Colin Banks has a significant interest in developing that area?"

"Colin?" Dan rubbed his chin. "No, I didn't know. But he invests in a lot of properties, so it doesn't surprise me. It's not something we've ever discussed, though."

"How well do you know him?"

"Are we veering into friend Charley territory now?"

"Grace can't find anything on him."

"Jeepers, Charley." Dan got up so fast he sent his rolling chair crashing against the wall. "You had Grace investigate him?"

"Not exactly. Lester Pyne did." She slid her hand underneath her pocketbook so he couldn't see her crossed fingers. It wasn't a lie, exactly. She had never asked Grace to look into the Banks family; Grace had done that for Charley on her own.

"Is it Colin or Meredith you're interested in?" He paced out from behind his desk, stopping in front of her.

She had to crane her neck to look up at him. "Believe it or not, I liked Meredith the couple of times I met her." That was true. She had wanted to hate the young woman but instead had been impressed by her poise and inner strength at each of their two encounters.

"She likes you, too. Keeps asking me to invite you to dinner."

"But you haven't."

He ran his hand through his hair, and she could have sworn she heard him curse. Except, Dan never cursed. "I've called you several times over the past few months. I thought I'd try to get you to meet me for coffee before I sprung dinner with Meredith on you. But I couldn't even swing that."

She stared down at her pocketbook and blinked away the tears that were welling in her eyes. "I'm sorry."

"Yeah, me too. Maybe some time though?" There was a waver of hope in his voice.

"Some time." She looked up and tried to smile.

"Okay. Colin." Dan returned to his desk. "I met him at the Liberal convention last summer and we hit it off. He's a recent immigrant looking to contribute to his new country, so he offered to help back my run in the next election."

"Do you know where his money comes from? Where he comes from?"

"He's originally from South Africa, but I don't know when he left. I do know he was in Europe during the war, although I'm not sure what he did. Meredith, I do know, was sent to school in Switzerland, for her protection. As for where his money comes from? Frankly, Charley, I never asked. I shouldn't have to tell you that talking about money is one of those taboo subjects we've been raised to avoid."

Boarding school in Switzerland. That explained why Meredith had no accent. Her South African pronunciation had probably been disciplined right out of her so she could sound as nondescript as every other proper young lady the school turned out.

"Don't you think you should know since he is supporting your campaign?" Charley asked.

He shrugged and she could tell by the firm set of his jaw

41

that, as far as he was concerned, the subject was closed. "Now, it's my turn to ask you some questions," he said, wiggling his eyebrows and grinning at her.

Her heart fluttered in her chest. Darn him, anyway. "Go ahead."

"I haven't seen your friend Mark Spadina around lately. My mother, for some unknown reason, wants to forge some sort of relationship with your disgraced-cop-turned-private-detective."

"He's not *my* anything! He's *your* half-brother."

"But he's no relation to either of my parents. We share a mother, who, it seems, neither of us knew."

Charley had had this discussion with Mark, too—when they'd been on speaking terms. Charley had grown up with a brother and, for good or ill, she understood there was a bond between siblings. Dan's parents, Rose and Edward, had come from large families, too. Dan and Mark, however, were each raised as only children—Dan in a loving family and Mark in a religious orphanage. Given the animosity between the two men, Charley was skeptical that they'd ever think of the other as a brother, but she understood why Rose was so determined to try.

"I haven't seen Detective Spadina in months," she said. "But his office is in your ward. If you want to know what he's up to, Alderman, you should pay him a visit."

Romeo Arcadi's taxi glided to a stop in front of the offices of the *Kingston Tribune*. The pleasant surprise of an exceptionally warm day was countered by the oppressive dankness brought on by the relentless rainfall. Charley thanked the cabbie for the ride and insisted she could open her own door. There was no reason for them both to become drenched.

She put her pocketbook into her satchel—she'd left her typewriter at the *Trib* yesterday—and braced herself to dash from the vehicle into the building. Her hand paused on the door's handle as she thought she recognized the two men standing under the canopy in front of the building. Lester Pyne, a plume of cigarette smoke swirling around him, she'd expect to see there. But not the other man.

"Mrs. Hall?" Romeo turned to look over his shoulder at her.

"Just give me a moment." She wiped at the condensation that had formed on the inside of the window.

It is him.

Why on earth was Constable Adams at the *Tribune*?

She watched them for a few more seconds. They were arguing about something. Adams was jabbing his finger menacingly into Lester's chest. She rolled down the window a crack to hear what they were saying but the deluge of rain hitting the roof of the taxi drowned them out.

Charley opened the door and backed out of the cab. She kept her head low when she turned toward the entrance, hoping the men would be too involved in their conversation to notice her.

"You've opened a real can of worms, you have," Adams barked. "I hope—" He stopped suddenly, glared at Charley, and then stalked off.

Lester dropped his cigarette butt onto the pavement and stubbed it out with the toe of his shoe. "Nasty day," he said, opening the door for her.

"What was Adams doing here?" Charley asked.

Lester shrugged. "Don't know. I was out having a smoke and he wandered by."

"You two seemed to be having a pretty heated conversation."

They'd barely entered the newsroom and already Lester had reached into his pocket to take out another cigarette. He placed it between his lips and flicked the lighter several times before the tip ignited. He took a puff and then replied. "He was busting my chops about how the press treats cops."

"Did it have anything to do with our story in today's early edition?" Charley had read the front-page article while at breakfast with Gran. As promised, Lester had included her name on the byline, but she wasn't sure he'd done her any favours. Once again, she'd been disappointed by the lack of human interest in Lester's writing. It had been a dry recounting of the facts. According to a source at City Hall, a group of investors—unnamed—wanted to purchase land west of the city for development and were lobbying for the city to annex it. The only thing that surprised her was the hotel proposal that Lester had told her about turned out to be nothing more than a plan to purchase one that already existed at the northwestern edge of the city. The source confirmed the proposal would be brought to the city council when it met next week.

"Nah, I'm not even sure he reads the papers himself." Lester hung his hat on the coat tree and began rolling up the sleeves of his shirt. The dampness from the outside had unpleasantly penetrated the old limestone building. "Thanks for your help on it, by the way. Much appreciated."

"Not that you used anything I gave you." She tried to temper her irritation but found she couldn't keep it at bay. "Why didn't you mention how Alderman Smythe's death paved the way for Carruthers and the others to push their pro-development agenda? Why didn't you name the investors?"

He stubbed out his cigarette and perched on the corner of his desk. "No proof. What we think happened to Smythe is conjecture on our part. We have nothing to connect his death to Carruthers. And as for who the investors are, what difference does it make? It's only relevant if we can find something fishy about Banks or one of the others, which we haven't."

"We may not have definitive proof, but I think we have enough to raise these issues in the minds of our readers."

"Not on the news pages."

"Don't you think readers have a right to know?"

"To know what? What you or I speculate may have happened? It's not news. Our job is to report the facts and let the reader make his own determination of what it means."

"That's a pretty narrow view of journalism," Charley

said. "Sometimes readers need our help to explain what things mean."

"I think you're doing readers a disservice. Providing opinion is the job of the editorialist. Reporters can't make themselves part of the story, not if we want to have any credibility."

"I disagree."

"I know you do." He started to reach for another cigarette but stopped himself, perhaps noticing her nose crinkle with displeasure. "Look, Hall, I get that you come from a family of self-made newspapermen. But that world of colourful commentary and overt political advocacy is dying—and good riddance to it. If we want to make a difference we can't be thought of as hacks or mouthpieces for the agendas of rich publishers. Schools have begun teaching principles of good journalism. We're developing codes of ethics, rules of practice. We are trying to create a respected profession."

"I think you are subverting the whole purpose of newspapers," she said.

"Not subverting: revolutionizing, changing with the times." He gave in to his tobacco craving and put a cigarette into his mouth, although he didn't light it. "Time marches on whether we like it or not. You can either rail against the injustice of it or you can accept it, become a part of it. Either way, it's going to happen."

Lester's words sat uncomfortably with Charley for the rest of the day and into the weekend. His comments about the changing role of reporters at newspapers could have as easily been uttered by her concerning the changing role of women in society. In fact, she was sure she'd used some of those same arguments when she'd pressed John Sherman to hire her at the *Trib*.

CHARLEY EXCUSED herself to Freddie and Evelyn and followed Bessie out of the dining room. Gran hadn't given her a choice, not that she'd wanted to stay at the breakfast table with their unwelcome visitor any longer than necessary.

Charley crossed the drawing room to her favourite chair, but Gran stopped her. "Come sit beside me on the sofa, please."

Charley eyed her grandmother with concern. Her long grey hair was still perfectly styled in its brioche-shaped bun and the lace collar of the ankle-length dress was perfectly starched, but her face looked pale and drawn. Her eyes, usually sparkling with life, were clouded and her lips were pursed in an unsuccessful attempt to conceal her displeasure.

Darn that Evelyn Pierrepont! And darn Freddie for inviting her.

Her maternal grandmother had returned from her cross-Canada sojourn late Friday afternoon and had immediately retired to her room, taking her dinner there. This morning, though, she'd marched into the dining room and began issuing orders to Rachel as though she was matron of the house.

Gran had said nothing.

Freddie, up early for once, had peppered Evelyn with questions about her train trip across the country and listened as though enraptured by her description of the changing colour of the foliage and the majesty of the mountains. It made Charley so mad to hear Evelyn speak as if they weren't already aware of the wonders of their own country.

It was an excruciating hour of Gran trying to be polite to the interloper while Freddie fawned over the woman. Charley pushed her eggs around on her plate but couldn't manage to eat anything. The few gulps of coffee she'd manage to swallow sat heavily in her stomach.

"It's going to be a very long four months," Charley said, leaning back against the cushions of the sofa and closing her eyes.

"It certainly will be if you don't improve your attitude," Bessie said.

"My attitude?" Her eyes flew open and she gaped at Gran.

"Your behaviour at breakfast was abhorrent, more like that of a spoilt child rather than the well-mannered young woman I raised, and I will not stand for it."

"Me? What about her? She struts around here like she owns the place."

"She is a guest and will be treated with respect."

"I don't see her showing you any respect."

Bessie took Charley's hand. "I appreciate that you think you are looking out for me, but it is unnecessary. I dare say I have had more experience handling the Evelyn Pierreponts of this world than you."

"But she comes across so imperial."

Bessie chuckled softly. "Well, she is a countess. Perhaps she can't help herself."

Charley frowned. "I keep remembering what you said about how she treated my mother when she married Father. How can a mother disown her own daughter?"

"I don't know. It broke poor Cynthia's heart." Bessie squeezed Charley's hand and then released it. "But that was many years ago. Perhaps she's realized her error and wants to make amends."

"If she has, it's because she needs Freddie to keep the title of Earl of Thorton in the family."

"In any event, I want you to keep in mind that your behaviour reflects on your grandfather and me and how we raised you. I will not give that woman any ammunition to claim superiority over me. Do you understand?"

Charley lowered her head. "Yes, Gran, of course."

Bessie stood. "Now, I need to go finish Mrs. Christie's *The Body in the Library* so Evelyn has time to read it before book club next week. I so enjoy Miss Marple's sleuthing."

"You're inviting her to join your book club?"

"Kindness not knives, remember?"

Charley moved over to her favourite chair, tucked her feet up under her, and picked up the morning's *Tribune*, which Rachel had left on the side table. She scanned the headlines. There was more about Louis St-Laurent replacing Mackenzie King as prime minister—it had happened at the beginning of the week, but after twenty-one years and 154 days in office, the extended coverage was warranted. The police had raided a building on Ontario Street last evening and found a gaming house in the basement. And there was a small article from the wire service about a protocol that had been signed in Paris by forty-seven countries to control the manufacture and distribution of potentially addictive drugs.

She flipped to her own section to make sure the print setter hadn't botched her instructions. *How to Dress Your Baby Like a Prince* was the lead story, followed by Alderman Delaney's impending nuptials. She'd compiled a list of Christmas markets that were planned for the next six weeks, and included a recipe for preparing the perfect holiday punch. John Sherman thought she was publishing the information prematurely, but Charley knew her readers were already preparing for the festive season.

"May I join you?"

Charley's breath caught at the sound of Evelyn's nasally accented voice from the doorway. *No!* she wanted to spit at her. She remembered Gran's reprimand, *kindness not knives*, and forced her jaw to unclench. "Of course." She straightened in her chair, lowered her feet to the floor, and then carefully folded the newspaper and returned it to the side table.

She watched as the woman who'd given birth to her mother—she couldn't think of her as Grandmama—crossed the room to choose the armchair closest to Charley. She'd put on weight since her arrival in Canada two months ago. She was still impossibly thin, but at least she no longer looked emaciated from her ocean crossing. Her face was sharp and angular, made to appear all the more so by the way she pulled her long, white hair off her face and tied it into a tight knot at the back of her head.

"I've asked Rachel to bring us some tea. I thought we could have a little chat."

"I'd prefer coffee," Charley said.

"Would you?" She seemed more intrigued than offended. "It's very American, isn't it? Coffee, I mean. I must say, I've never quite understood the attraction, but there you have it."

"Maybe it's a colonial thing," Charley said sarcastically.

"Hmm, perhaps. It's originally from Ethiopia—Abyssinia, as it was once known." Her brow furrowed. "But to my knowledge, that country was never part of the Empire."

Charley had had enough of this mindless chit-chat. *Sorry Gran.* "Why are you here?"

"Do you mean here, in this drawing room with you now? Or do you mean in Canada?" Before Charley could reply she said, "I am with you because you are my grand-daughter and I'd like to get to know you. And I believe I've already explained why I am in Canada."

"To convince Freddie to go back to England with you."

"To assume his rightful title." She paused while Rachel set out the tea service and prepared the two cups. After she'd left, Evelyn continued. "Don't you want him to claim his family's legacy?"

Her brother had spent a lifetime avoiding the Stormont legacy, why would he want to embrace a Pierrepont one? But it wasn't the pitting of one family against the other that disturbed her.

"The male legacy, you mean," Charley said, bitterly. "You had no trouble casting out your daughter. Don't you think it's ironic that it's her son you now so desperately need."

"Life has a way of teaching the hardest of lessons." Evelyn stared down into her cup.

"Are you saying you regret the way you treated my mother?"

"I regret a lot of things. But to your point, yes, there is not a day that goes by that I don't miss Cynthia. But I'm comforted by the certainty that I'll see her again soon, and I can make amends then."

Evelyn's statement took her by surprise. *See her again soon?* Was she ill? Charley leaned forward. The woman's eyes did seem somewhat cloudy and her wrinkled cheeks looked hollow and grey.

"Oh, don't get lost in fanciful thoughts," Evelyn chided her. "All I mean is that I am approaching my eightieth year and one cannot expect to live forever."

"I did some research after you first arrived. Your son died in '21 from Spanish flu and your husband not long afterward. Why wait so long before coming for Freddie?"

"What has your grandmother told you?"

Charley frowned. Growing up, Gran and Grandpa had told her and Freddie very little about their parents. She'd assumed it was simply too painful, and it probably was. Once she started working at the *Tribune*, Charley had researched all she could about Cynthia and Frederick Stormont II, but it had only been recently—while investigating their murders—that Gran had revealed that her mother had been born an aristocrat. "She told me that after my parents died, you came here to try to take Freddie and me back to England with you."

"I see." She sounded guarded.

"Do you deny it?"

A furrow formed between her well-plucked eyebrows. "What you've been told isn't completely accurate, no."

"Then what is?"

Evelyn put down her teacup. "After I learned of Cynthia's death, I did come to Kingston. Your grandparents were very welcoming, despite the estrangement that had existed between my daughter and me. I am sure you and Freddie don't remember, but I took you for walks along the lake's shore that autumn. It was a very healing time for me. You see, my son and husband had died a few years previously. With Cynthia gone I had no one."

Charley's tea had cooled beyond her liking. She put her cup down on top of the newspaper. She felt her icy reserve toward Evelyn begin to thaw. What must she have been thinking? By the mid 1920s, both she and Gran had lost all their children, but Bessie at least still had Grandpa. Maybe Evelyn's desire to gain custody of her grandchildren had been motivated by feelings of loneliness rather than entitlement. "Was that why you wanted Freddie and me to go back to England with you."

Evelyn swallowed heavily, then raised her gaze to stare unwaveringly into Charley's eyes. "Not you."

Charley couldn't wait for Monday to arrive so she could return to work. She was desperate to get away from Evelyn Pierrepont and her two devastating words.

Not you.

Her maternal grandmother hadn't tried to explain—not even to pretend that leaving one child with Gran and Grandpa would be an honourable thing to do—and she hadn't expressed remorse. Evelyn Pierrepont hadn't wanted Charley. It was that simple and that horrible.

Gran had seemed nonplussed when Charley pressed her on it. She said they would never have allowed Charley or Freddie or both of them to be taken back to England, so it didn't matter what Evelyn had wanted.

Except it did to Charley.

"You're here early," Grace said as Charley entered the newsroom. "Must be something in the water."

"What do you mean?" Charley asked.

Grace cocked her head toward the centre of the room where Lester Pyne was furiously typing away.

"Hi Lester," Charley said. "What are you working on?"

He typed to the end of the sentence, stubbed out the cigarette that had been hanging from his lips, and then looked over his shoulder at her. "I'm trying to get a few stories in the hopper. I need to leave early today."

"Is everything okay?" He didn't look well. His face was pale, and it looked like he'd done nothing more than run his fingers through his thinning blond hair.

"No. Linda took off on the weekend, and Eleanor's a bit under the weather so she's going to need me to help with Anthony."

"Is Linda coming back? Or what about Emerson? Can't he help with the baby?"

Pyne turned back to his typewriter. "I don't know." He started typing again.

"Why don't you tell me what you're working on? Maybe I can finish it up for you."

Lester rolled his chair back and swivelled it around to look at her. "You'd do that?"

"Well sure." Charley had met enough working mothers to know that finding reliable help with their children was a challenge. She was impressed with Lester's willingness to pitch in. Most fathers she knew felt that childrearing was women's work.

"Okay, I've been working on the death of Raymond Palmer over the weekend."

"Palmer's dead?" That shook her. She'd seen him a few days ago in Dan's office. "How?"

"Officially, he drowned."

"Officially? You don't believe that?"

Lester rubbed his hands over his bleary eyes. "Apparently, he was hiking in the marshlands west of the city. Alone. Slipped and fell down an embankment. They figure he knocked his head on a rock or something. He was discovered in less than a foot of water."

Charley recalled Palmer as a fit man in his late forties, but if he'd been unconscious when he fell into the water.... "It was a nice weekend. A late fall hike doesn't seem all that unreasonable."

"I think it was a message."

A message?

Charley felt the urge to pace. Thoughts came clearer to her when she was moving. Instead, she shifted her weight from foot to foot.

Think, Charley.

"Okay, so Palmer was found out near the area the investors want annexed. And he worked in the planning department for the city." It was tenuous but she could maybe make the case for it being suspicious. "But what is the message and who's it for?"

"Palmer was my source at City Hall."

Less tenuous. "But there was nothing in your article that was controversial," Charley said.

"There must have been *something*."

"Or his death over the weekend could be nothing more than a coincidence."

Lester shrugged. "Maybe I'm being paranoid."

Charley wasn't fond of coincidences. Working with Mark had taught her that they were rare—especially when it came to murder. "I can reach out to my contacts at the police department and see if they'll tell me anything more. Is there going to be an autopsy?"

"I already spoke to the cops. They're convinced it's an accident. The body's already been released to his family."

"I ran into Palmer at Dan Cannon's office last week. Dan said it had nothing to do with the west-end development proposal, but I could talk to him again, see if he thinks there was anything unusual about the proposal and take it from there."

Lester stood and grabbed his hat from the coat tree near his desk. "I appreciate this, Hall. Thanks for being such a pal." He shrugged on his woolen overcoat and knotted a scarf around his neck. "And tell Sherman it's a joint byline, okay?"

———

"Is he in?"

Diana Huff arched an eyebrow and gazed at Charley with irritation. "I guess the courtesy of making an appointment was a one-time event."

"I need to see him."

"Of course you do. But he's in a meeting and he's booked up all day. I can have him call you when he gets a spare moment if you like."

Charley blew out her frustration and sat down on the chair across from Diana's desk. "I'll wait." It wasn't that she didn't believe Dan's secretary when she said her boss was booked up all day, but the woman loved playing gatekeeper a little too much. Charley knew from experience that Dan would make time for her; Diana did too, and it drove her crazy. "So, are you involved in planning the wedding?" Charley asked, happy to pass the time by stirring the pot.

"That's the purview of the bride."

"I thought that with Dan being so busy, both here and at the shipyard, that you'd be consulted."

Diana's face flushed pink but the door to Dan's office swung open before she could reply. Charley jumped to her feet and started for the door. She stopped, startled to see Constables Marillo and Adams exiting the office.

"Mrs. Hall?" Marillo took a step back in surprise, almost backing into Adams.

"Charley, what are you doing here?" Dan said, following the men into the outer office.

"I came to see you." She turned to Marillo. "Why are the police here?"

"Routine business. We're following up on the raid that took place over the weekend," Marillo said.

"Raid?"

"It was in your paper," Adams sneered.

Oh, yes, the gaming den.

"The Tassisti Social Club is in my ward," Dan explained.

"Then you're not here about Raymond Palmer's death?" Charley asked Marillo. She was going to pretend Adams didn't exist.

Marillo turned back and held out his hand to Dan. "Thank you for your help, Alderman." He turned and nodded to Charley, "Mrs. Hall," and walked past her, followed by Adams.

"I'll be right back," Charley said to Dan and followed the officers out into the hallway. "Wait, please," she called to them.

Adams kept walking, but Marillo stopped and turned back. With a sigh Adams did the same. "I suppose if we don't talk to you now, you'll tag along wherever we go, pestering us until we do," the older constable said.

"Probably," she conceded. "I wanted to ask you about Palmer's death."

"Palmer?" Adams snapped. "What about it? It was an accident." He started to move on, but Marillo put a hand on his arm to stop him.

"Why are you asking about it?" Marillo asked. "Is there something we should know?"

"Did you investigate it?"

"I did," Adams said. "He drowned while hiking in the marshlands."

Charley turned to Marillo. "And you? Were you there?"

He shook his head. "No, it was a weekend. Adams did it alone."

Again?

"You don't think it's suspicious that the official responsible for preparing the planning department's recommendation on a controversial plan to annex part of Kingston Township drowns at the very site of where it's being proposed?"

"Well..." Marillo hesitated.

"Oh, for heaven's sake, it was an accident. He was likely out there as part of writing his recommendation. Don't go stirring up trouble where there is none." Adams scowled at Charley before looking for support from his partner. When Marillo didn't say anything, he stalked off in a huff.

"You agree, Palmer's death is suspicious?" Charley asked.

Marillo had been watching his partner's retreat. He turned his gaze back to Charley. "Only the timing, but if Adams says it's an accident that's good enough for me."

"He has no one to corroborate his findings. And don't forget, he investigated Alderman Smythe's fall and ruled it an accident, too. Smythe's death is the reason the proposal—"

"Stop right there! I'd think very carefully before you start making accusations against a member of the Kingston Police Department, Mrs. Hall."

She had seen Constable Marillo in various moods from exasperation to irritation—she'd generally been the cause of them—but never, in the years she'd known him, had she ever seen him angry. She took a step back as a dark red mask descended over his face and his usually warm hazel eyes turned to hard, dark orbs of menace. "I'm sorry," she said quickly. "Sometimes I get carried away with a story. I didn't mean to cast aspersions on Constable Adams' character or Kingston PD."

And then he was back to being the same old Constable Marillo she knew. "Okay," he said quietly. "Let's forget all about it."

"Can I ask you about the raid, then?" If the Palmer story wasn't going to pan out, perhaps there was another story here.

"What do you want to know? It's all in the report down at the station."

"It was supposed to be a social club, but you found gambling there?"

He nodded.

"Is that a big deal? Unusual?"

"We're starting to see an alarming upsurge in organized gambling that's being carried out in premises ostensibly occupied and operated by incorporated social clubs. The real operators, though, are professional gamblers. It's become such a concern that the provincial police have set up an entire branch dedicated to stopping it. You know, you should talk to your friend Mark Spadina. It started in Toronto, so I bet he knows all about it."

Mark again. She had no intention of talking to him about anything. It didn't matter than he was a former Toronto Police detective. She'd get whatever information she needed somewhere else.

"Who conducted the raid? Kingston PD or this new anti-gambling group?" she asked.

"We did, at their request."

"And what is Alderman Cannon's involvement? Why were you here to see him?"

"You're a good reporter, Mrs. Hall. Persistent. I'd like to say I miss you on the city beat, but frankly, my life is easier with you doing the women's pages." He chuckled. "As the alderman said, we were here to talk to him because the building where the raid took place is in his ward. Now, if you'll excuse me, I have a few feathers to unruffle with my partner."

Charley walked past Diana's desk, ignoring her indignant cry of complaint, and strode into Dan's office. She didn't knock. She knew he was alone.

He glanced up from his desk and with a resigned sigh, motioned for her to take a chair across from him. "Are you here for business or personal reasons?" he asked.

He looked haggard. His sandy brown hair was sticking out from all angles, a telltale sign he'd been running his hands through it. It meant he was upset.

"It was supposed to be business, but you don't look so good. Is something wrong?" she asked, genuinely concerned. She knew he held two very demanding jobs—city alderman and legal counsel for his family's shipbuilding company—but he usually navigated both easily thanks to his good humour and a strong work ethic. "Are things okay with Meredith?"

His bloodshot eyes grew round and he blinked rapidly. "Why do you ask?"

Oh, dear. She was the last person who should be giving him romantic advice. "You seem too upset for it to be about work."

"Well, it's a bit of both, I'm afraid." He stood and circled the desk, collapsing into the chair beside her.

"Is it related to the police raid? To Raymond Palmer's death?"

Dan cocked his head to the side and gave her a shadow of his movie-star grin. "You're fishing, Reporter Hall."

"Am I close?"

He leaned back, closed his eyes and raked his hands through his hair. "On or off the record?" He opened his eyes and turned to her. "Never mind. It doesn't matter. It's going to be a matter of public record, anyway. I'd rather talk to you than your replacement."

"Lester's not such a bad egg," she said.

He sat forward. "That's a surprise."

She shrugged. "He's growing on me."

"Well, still, I'm glad it's you here and not him." Dan stood and walked back to his chair behind his desk. "The police were here, not as a courtesy because the raid took place in my ward but because Colin Banks' name appears on the Tassisti Social Club's charter. They wanted to know what I knew about him before they went to question him." He leaned forward. "The thing is, I already knew Colin was about to be brought in for questioning. He called me early this morning and asked me to represent him, which of course, I can't do. I'm not that kind of lawyer. So, I made some calls and got him a good one."

"Marillo says those social clubs are fronts for organized gambling. If Banks' name is on the charter—"

"I know." He looked miserable. "I should have taken you more seriously when you asked me about him last week. But I swear, Charley, I've never seen the man do anything crooked. I had no reason to suspect—"

"You still don't know he's dirty," Charley said to ease his anxiety even though it didn't look good for Banks.

"He swears he's not, that his name is on the charter because he owns the building and the social club organizers needed someone of his stature to get their application approved by the province."

"It could be true." Charley couldn't believe she was the one defending Banks.

"But it makes me realize how little I know about him."

"And Meredith."

Dan nodded. "And Meredith."

"Let's not borrow trouble, okay," Charley said. "Why don't we wait to see what the police find out. He hasn't been charged with anything yet, has he?"

"No. And you're right. He's been a good friend and supporter, and I can't imagine Meredith being complicit in anything disreputable. Thank you."

Again, that dazzling smile. Charley looked down at her hands so he couldn't see how he could still affect her.

"So, what was it you originally came here for?" Dan asked. "It wasn't the raid, I don't think."

"No, I wanted to ask you about Raymond Palmer. He was here when I came to see you last week."

"Yeah, and ironically, we were discussing the provincial police's concern about organized gambling coming to Kingston and what the city could do to stop it. He was giving me a head's-up about the planned raid on the social club since it's in my district."

"How did he know about it?"

"Seems he's the one who tipped off the police as to what was going on there."

Charley's mind was in a whirlwind. What if they had this all wrong? What if Palmer's death had nothing to do with the proposed development, after all? Maybe it was a coincidence—that hated word—that his body had been found in the marshland off Gardiners Road. Wouldn't it make more sense that his death was connected to the arrival of a crime group from Toronto and the police raid on the Tassisti Social Club?

"You could be a little more appreciative," Charley said. Honestly, the man acted as if she'd committed a heinous crime. She'd done as he'd asked and put both their names on the article.

"We've talked about this," Lester said. "Personal opinion has no place in a news story. It's one thing for you to do it on your own pages, but to do it under my byline..." His face had taken on a dark, ruddy hue and his pale blue eyes seemed to pop out. If he wasn't careful, he was going to collapse from apoplexy.

"Indeed, she didn't come out and say Raymond Palmer's death was connected to the social club raid," John Sherman said, attempting to mediate the argument. He'd called the pair into his office as soon as the yelling had started in the newsroom.

"She might as well have." Lester waved last evening's edition of the *Trib* in front of Charley's face. "You've drawn a pretty straight line from the arrival of criminal elements in the city to the raid on the social club, to Palmer's role in raising the alarm and his, and I quote, 'dubitable death by drowning'."

"Well, we all agree, it was dubitable, don't we?" She glanced between the two men. "I would think you'd be relieved, Lester. If Palmer's death isn't connected to the west-end development proposal, then it's not related to the story you wrote about it. Any *message*, if there was one, was meant for someone else."

"I suppose there is that," he conceded and collapsed down onto the couch. "But you have to understand, that kind of reporting goes against everything I believe a journalist to be. I can't have my name associated with it."

"I understand and it won't happen again." Sherman turned to Charley. "Right, Hall?"

She shrugged. "You're the editor."

"Yes, I am." Sherman nodded, satisfied, and returned to his position of power behind his elevated desk. "What's the next step? I think you two should go see Colin Banks and find out why his name is on that social club's charter. The police questioned him but didn't take him into custody. I think we need to get his side of the story, and then follow up with the cops to see why he's still a free man."

"Not the two of us," Lester said. "I don't need a partner on this."

"But I can get us in to see Banks," Charley said, fearing her short time back on the city beat was about to be terminated. She wasn't sure Colin Banks would want to see her, especially since she was responsible for sending his wife to jail, but she could prevail on him as a long-time friend of Dan's or exploit her Stormont pedigree. And if all of those failed, there was always his sister, Meredith. Dan had said his *fiancée* wanted to get to know her better. She knew this wasn't quite what the woman had in mind, but she was desperate to stay on the story.

"Okay, the two of you," Sherman said.

"But—" Lester started to protest.

"But Lester approves the final copy," Sherman said to appease him.

⸻

"CHARLEY! LESTER!" Grace called across the newsroom.

"We're on a story," Charley called back. "We'll talk to you later."

"Are you going to see Colin Banks? You need to hear this first."

"How did she know where we were going?" Lester muttered as he returned his hat and coat to the coat tree and followed Charley into Grace's morgue.

"She knows everything that goes on here," Charley whispered. "You can't keep secrets from Grace."

"That's right so don't even try." Grace grinned at them. "Tea?"

"No. Whaddaya got?" Lester was brusque.

Grace's eyebrows rose and she threw Charley a questioning look.

"He's anxious to see what Banks has to say," Charley said. She was anxious, too, but knew better than to rush her friend. The woman was a genius when it came to research. If she said she had information they needed to hear before interviewing Banks, Charley wasn't going to dispute her. And if she wanted to serve you tea first, well you accepted it with a smile knowing it was the price to pay for excellence.

Who'd have ever thought she would be the patient one. She'd have to tell Mark, he'd—

Darn it.

"I think I'll pass on the tea, too," Charley said. "With Evelyn visiting from England, I've had more than enough tea to last me a while."

"How is that going?" Grace asked. "Freddie seems excited to have her here."

"Ladies, please! Can we get to the point?" Lester said in exasperation.

"Oh, all right." Grace heaved an exaggerated sigh of resignation. "I know who Colin Banks is."

"Isn't he Colin Banks?" Charley asked.

"Nope. His real name is Christo Van Blerk." She turned to Lester. "And you're right, he is South African."

"And his sister? Is she his sister?" Charley asked, starting to feel real concern for Dan.

"Merisse Van Blerk, and yes, she's his sister. Actually, it was through her that I found them." Grace picked up a file folder, plucked out a piece of paper and handed it to Charley.

It was a grainy copy of a page from a school yearbook. A dozen squares were arrayed in three rows of four, each containing the face of a young woman. Charley recognized Meredith's face immediately despite the strange name typed beneath it.

"The information that Alderman Cannon gave you about her going to school in Switzerland during the war was how I tracked them down," Grace said.

"Did they come into the country legally?" Lester asked.

"Yes, but I don't think they were vetted all that thoroughly." Grace handed Charley another photo.

Charley stared down at an older man who bore a striking resemblance to Col—Christo Van Blerk. There was a menacing-looking coat of arms stitched onto his breast pocket. "Who's this?"

"Ah, that's Caspar Van Blerk, their father."

"And the coat of arms? The eagle and insignia look German, like the emblem of the Nazi Reich."

"That's the problem. It essentially is. He's wearing the seal of the *Ossewabrandwag.*"

"The what?"

"The *Ossewabrandwag,*" Lester said. "It was a pro-German organization that opposed South Africa's support of the Allies. It had a paramilitary arm, *Stormjaers*, who engaged in sabotage against the South African government. They blew up electrical power lines and railroads and they cut telegraph and telephone lines. The government cracked down on the organization and sent a lot of its members to internment camps for the duration of the war." He turned to Grace. "The *Ossewabrandwag* doesn't exist anymore."

"No, you're right," she said. "Most Afrikaners thought it had gone too far and, by the end of the war, it had been absorbed into the far-right National Party. Caspar Van Blerk was never imprisoned, but it's recorded that he committed suicide in May 1945, after the fall of Berlin."

"Do you have any photos of Christo?" Charley asked.

"These are the only two I've got."

"So, do we assume Christo was a member of the *Ossewabrandwag* because his father was?" Charley asked. "Dan said he'd been in Europe during the war. Maybe he was there fighting for the Allies?"

"It is possible. Some fought in Italy, but by far the majority of South Africans fought in Africa," Lester said.

"And with the RAF," Charley said, acknowledging what Lester had first told her. "You said some of the flyers were from Johannesburg."

"There's more," Grace said. "The Van Blerks owned diamond mines."

"Holy moly." Lester leapt off his stool and spun around.

"What does that mean?" Charley asked.

"There were all kinds of stories of diamonds being

smuggled into Europe to fund the Jerries," Lester explained. "You're sure Cannon said Banks was in Europe, not England?"

"Yeah, why?"

"Because if he was working for the Allies, he would have taken the diamonds to England where the high command was," Grace said.

"Hold on. We don't know that he brought diamonds at all," Charley said.

"No, but think about it," Grace countered. "He arrives in Canada and changes his name. I can't find any immigration information for either Banks or Van Blerk. I even checked under his sister's name. *Nada.* But when he arrives, he has enough money with him to buy a mansion on Front Road and half of downtown Kingston."

"He's using diamonds," Charley said.

"Dirty diamonds left over from the Nazis," Lester spat. "And that's probably what he's using to fund his investment in the west-end development, too."

And Dan's political dreams.

CHARLEY ACCEPTED Romeo Arcadi's hand as she stepped out of his cab. Dan was already waiting for them in the driveway of Banks' impressive three-story limestone mansion.

"What are you doing here?" Lester asked as he came around the taxi.

A confused expression crossed Dan's face and Charley said, "I asked him."

"What? Why would you do that? Lester's outraged voice was chased by a barking cough. He reached into his pocket for a cigarette.

"I wouldn't," Dan said. "Not if you're wanting to talk to Colin. He doesn't like the smell and will probably send you away."

Charley watched Arcadi's cab back down the driveway and onto the street. She turned back to Lester. "If it's you and me, Banks could easily dismiss our questions or refuse to answer them. He can't do that so easily if Dan's here."

"So nice to be your stalking horse once again, Mrs. Hall," Dan said dryly.

"Does she do this to you often?" Lester asked.

"More than I care to admit."

"I am starting to see why you're so popular down at the police station, Hall," Lester said sarcastically.

"What have you heard?" Charley asked.

"Just that you can be a bit of a bull in a china shop with your single-minded determination to get answers."

"Take no prisoners," Dan said sharing a grin with Lester.

Single-minded determination to get answers. Well, that wasn't so bad. Charley had been afraid the complaints might have been more of a sexist nature. She sometimes got a sense some of the officers were uncomfortable dealing with a woman. "It's what makes me such a good reporter," she said.

"It can be a little hard on your friends, though," Dan said.

She threw him a sharp glance, but he was still smiling. "Nothing you can't handle, Alderman." She winked at him. It was almost like the old days when they were best friends and their relationship had been free and easy. She missed him. She missed them. It would never be the same now that he was to marry Meredith, but she was relieved that they could still share these small moments of familiarity.

"Are you here to see Miss Banks?" the housekeeper asked recognizing Dan.

"Not this time, Mrs. Harper," he replied. "We're here to see Mr. Banks. We don't have an appointment, unfortunately."

"Oh, I'm sure that won't be necessary." She took their coats. "Go wait in the library and I'll fetch him."

Charley glanced around the library with its glorious floor-to-ceiling wooden bookshelves and comfortable chairs and couches. It was her third time in this room. She hoped she fared better today than the previous two occasions.

"Dan! Good to see you as always." Colin Banks wasn't a big man, but he had a force of personality that commanded the room as soon as he entered it. He would have made a formidable politician himself. "And I see you've brought guests." He turned to Charley and Lester. "Mrs. Hall, a pleasure to finally meet you. And I'm afraid I don't know this other gentleman."

"Lester Pyne, city reporter with the *Kingston Tribune*," Lester said extending his hand.

"I recognize the name. Welcome." Banks shook his hand and then indicated they should all take a seat. If he was surprised at the arrival of two reporters, he didn't show it. "Can I get you anything? Tea? Coffee? Something stronger?"

Charley had been about to ask for coffee as subjects tended to be more forthcoming when they were at ease, and sharing a drink was a social activity. Unfortunately, Lester beat her to it and refused, and to make matters worse, he immediately took out his notepad and pencil.

Honestly, could the man's manners be any worse?

As she feared, Banks' demeanor immediately changed. He sat up straight in his chair and his expression became guarded.

She threw Dan a desperate look, but he simply shrugged his shoulders. They were on their own.

"I'd like to ask you about your involvement in the Tassisti Social Club," Lester began.

"I thought as much." Was it her imagination or did Banks seem to relax a tad? "You obviously heard through your sources at the police station that I was brought in for questioning? Yes?"

"Your name was on the club's charter."

"Yes. And as I explained to the police, I was aiding a

tenant. I had no idea he was planning to use the premises to set up a gambling den."

"How were you aiding your tenant?" Charley asked.

"I am new to your country, Mrs. Hall, so I am not sure how the laws work. But my understanding was my tenant was taking over the social club's charter from someone else. It was required to have the names of sureties for the application to your provincial government."

"What sort of surety were you providing? Character?" Lester said.

"Absolutely not! It was financial. I verified that the gentleman had been a good tenant—always paid his rent on time. I said nothing about his character. And I didn't know that my letter to the minister would result in my name being included on the charter."

"Where is this tenant now?" Charley asked. "He wasn't among those rounded up in the raid." There had been a dozen or so men arrested for being found in a betting house, but none of them had been on the charter's list of directors. As far as she knew, Banks was the only person named on the charter who'd been brought in for questioning. The rest were still at large.

Banks shrugged. "I don't know. As I told the police, I've seen him twice—once when he rented the building and the second time when he asked me to write the letter to the provincial minister."

"How does he pay his rent?" Charley asked.

"A cheque arrives in the mail every month."

"From him?" Charley asked.

"Not from him personally, no. It comes from a business account. That's standard for most of the companies I rent to."

"Well, that's that, then." Dan slapped his knees and

stood, obviously relieved that his friend had a satisfactory explanation.

"Not quite," Lester said. "I have a few more questions for Mr. Banks."

"In that case, I am going to have a drink." Dan walked over to the sideboard. "Anyone else? No?" He poured himself a generous portion of whiskey and returned to his seat.

"We were looking into your background," Lester said.

"It's the type of story our readers love," Charley added quickly, more for Dan's benefit than for Banks'. She didn't want him to think their investigation had been personally motivated. "You are new to town and have quickly become a prominent member of the community."

"And you couldn't find anything." Banks sounded unconcerned. "It's not uncommon. Many records were destroyed during the war. Many people were displaced."

"But there is usually some record of immigration," Charley said. "Since we couldn't find anything, perhaps you can tell us about yourself?"

"Let's start with the *Ossewabrandwag*," Lester declared.

Oh, for heaven's sake! And the police have the nerve to suggest I'm like a bull in a china shop?

"The Oss-what?" Dan said.

"*Ossewabrandwag*," Banks said easily. "I am familiar with the organization. Given my accent, I can hardly pretend to be from anywhere other than South Africa, can I?"

"Were you a member?" Charley asked.

"No."

"But your father was, wasn't he, *Christo*?" Lester asked.

"Who is Christo?" Dan rocketed out of his chair,

spilling a sizable amount of his whiskey onto the woolen carpet.

Banks waved him back into his seat. He was a cool cucumber, Charley would give him that. Either he had nothing to hide or he was the best actor she'd ever seen. If Lester had been a bit more subtle in his questioning she might have been able to figure out which.

"I am...was Christo, my friend. Christo Van Blerk," he said to Dan before turning to Lester. "And yes, my father was a member of the *Ossewabrandwag*, back in Johannesburg. My compliments on your research skills. We could have used you during the war."

"On whose side?" Lester said.

Banks smiled. "South Africa was aligned with the Allies."

"But the *Ossewabrandwag* supported the Nazis," Lester pressed

"And when it was outlawed, my father was stripped of his land and jailed," Banks said.

"But not you. You spent most of the war in Europe," Lester said. "Your family owned diamond mines. Did you bring diamonds to Hitler?"

Dan had visibly paled. He gulped down the last of his drink and looked longingly toward the sideboard for more, but he didn't move.

Banks stood. "This interrogation is at an end."

"Answer the question, dammit!" Lester leapt to his feet, his face red with indignation "Did you provide diamonds to the enemy."

Banks headed for the door, pausing to place a hand on Dan's shoulder as he passed his chair. "I am sorry, my friend." He continued out the door. "You may show yourselves out."

Dan's face had taken on a greenish tint and he looked as if he was going to be physically ill. He buried his face in his hands. "What have you done?"

"I'm sorry, Dan, but isn't it better that you know now?" Charley's heart broke for him. She hated hurting him, but Banks had been lying to him. Imagine if this information came out in the middle of his election campaign?

"Know what exactly?" Dan asked, looking up at her. "You have no proof of any wrong-doing."

"He lied about his name?" Charley said.

"Oh, I don't know, *Mrs. Hall.*" He stood and glared at her. "There are all kinds of reasons people choose to adopt new names. It doesn't mean they are criminals?"

"I realize this comes as a rather unpleasant surprise, Alderman, but—" Lester said.

Dan whirled on him. "And you! You're worse than she is." He turned back to Charley. "You know, Charley, I used to think your myopic outlook on life was a quirk of your character; that you weren't using me, just including me as an unsuspecting co-conspirator in one or another of your intrigues; that regardless of how self-serving your actions seemed, your heart was in the right place."

"It is," she whispered.

"I'm not so sure anymore." He cast his gaze over her shoulder as if he couldn't bear to look at her. "I knew you were unhappy about my engagement to Meredith, but never in my wildest dreams did I ever imagine you were so vengeful that you would try to ruin her life like this."

CHARLEY LEFT Lester waiting for a taxi on Banks' front step and walked down the driveway onto Front Road. Twilight fell early in November and it would be dark before she made it back to the *Trib*, but she needed to walk. She had a lot to think about.

Lester's aggression toward Banks had seemed out of character for a reporter who refused to make himself part of the story. In hindsight, though, she should have anticipated how he'd react—what it would be like for a soldier, who'd seen the carnage of war first-hand, to come face-to-face with an enemy collaborator.

Possible enemy collaborator.

They had no proof. If they'd gone in with a plan, they might have been able to get more information out of Banks —backed him into a corner, tricked him into confessing. She'd done it before, countless times. But today, they'd allowed their excitement to get the better of them and had gone in unprepared. All they'd succeeded in getting was an acknowledgment that Christo Van Blerk had changed his name to Colin Banks. And that wasn't a crime. Heck, it wasn't even a story.

She lingered on the corner of Days Road to consider whether she wanted to turn north toward the *Tribune* or continue along Front Road until it turned into King Street West, and home. The sun had pretty much set and there was a damp chill in the air. Home would be so easy... Except it didn't feel much like home these days. Not with Evelyn there. She turned up the collar of her coat and headed north.

She tried to block out the look on Dan's face as he accused her of a vendetta against Meredith, but she couldn't shake it. His reaction had surprised her as much as Lester's. She thought he'd be furious to learn Banks' real identity and family connection with the pro-German *Ossewabrandwag*. It could sink his political aspirations. But instead, his concern had been for Meredith—

Darn it!

She whirled around. She had to go back. Dan was assuming his *fiancée* was an innocent in all this. But she'd changed her name, too, so she couldn't be.

Could she?

She hesitated and then resumed her journey to the *Tribune*. Dan was convinced she was out to ruin his engagement. It wasn't true but going back with more accusations would add fuel to that fallacy. She'd give him some time to calm down and try to talk to him again.

Beep. Beep.

Charley jumped as a dark sedan honked its horn and pulled to a stop in front of her. She hesitated, not sure if she should run or prepare to fight. She was getting ready to scream when she recognized Romeo Arcadi's capped head sticking out the driver's window.

"How did you know where I was?" she asked, sliding gratefully into the back seat.

"Mr. Pyne told me. So, after I dropped him off at the newspaper, I circled back to pick you up. I figured with the dark and cold, you'd have had enough of a walk." He winked at her in the rear-view mirror, then shifted gears and eased back onto the road.

"Thank you." She leaned back against the leather headrest.

"You should be more careful," he chided her. "A young woman shouldn't be out walking alone at night."

"It's not even five o'clock."

"Still, it's dark. You never know."

Charley wanted to argue with him. The streets of Kingston were safe, and she was often out after dark. But she had to concede this was an area she wasn't familiar with —and her heart was only now settling back into her chest after her initial fright.

"Tough story?" Arcadi glanced at her from the mirror.

His question surprised her. He never asked about what she was working on. If he had any comment at all, it had to do with his displeasure at some address or another he was taking her to. The truth was, she resisted talking to him about anything much because the conversation usually ended up with Arcadi suggesting he arrange a meeting between her and his unmarried son. She blamed Gran for that. Somehow the two had become friendly and, at some point, Gran had disclosed that Theo had been missing since the raid on Dieppe in 1942.

"It's a story," she said.

"Mr. Pyne seemed particularly upset when I picked him up. Did you two argue about the alderman? Or perhaps it was your meeting with Mr. Banks?"

Mercifully, they'd arrived in front of the *Tribune*. She thanked Arcadi and mumbled an excuse about needing to talk to Lester. The cab driver's questions were out of character. Odd. But she didn't have time to ponder it at the moment.

"Charley!" Grace rushed across the newsroom as soon as she saw her. "What on earth happened?" She nodded toward Lester who was sitting at his desk, head lowered and pounding furiously on his typewriter.

"Banks admitted he changed his name but denies any involvement with gambling at the Tassisti Social Club."

"And the diamonds?"

Charley shook her head. She looped her arm through Grace's and guided her toward Lester's desk. He gave no indication that he noticed them waiting behind him. Charley peered over his shoulder, her eyes widening with surprise at what she was seeing. She picked up two already completed pages off his desk and began to read them. Even by her somewhat looser standards of journalism—according to Lester—she'd never publish this. It was libelous. He was outright accusing Colin Banks of smuggling diamonds into Europe to help the Nazis and then buying properties in Canada to hide the source of his fortune and orchestrating the murders of two men who were getting in his way.

Lester pulled the last page from his typewriter, rolled his chair back, and stood.

"You can't publish this," Charley said.

Lester took the sheets of paper from her, tapped them together on his desk to straighten them. Then he carefully ripped them in half, and half again, before dropping them into his wastepaper basket. "I feel better now."

"I don't understand," Charley said.

"Of course we can't publish that. I just needed to get it down on paper for myself. You walk to organize your thoughts, I write." Lester gave her a sheepish smile. "I owe you an apology for my behaviour at Banks' house this afternoon."

"No apology required," she said. "It must have been difficult to be in the same room with a man we suspect of helping the Nazis."

"Still, it was unprofessional of me."

"What's next?" Grace asked.

"I'll keep digging until I find something that won't land us in hot water facing charges of libel." The phone on Lester's desk rang and he reached to pick up the receiver. "Pyne."

Charley and Grace had started to walk away but turned back when they thought they heard Lester gagging and a loud thump. He had collapsed beside his desk, all colour drained from his already pale face. He'd dragged the telephone down with him and the receiver was still clutched in his hand.

Is he having a stroke? Charley remembered what her grandfather had looked like when she'd come upon him after his first stroke. "Call a doctor," she yelled.

"No," Lester managed to get the word out.

Grace took the receiver from him while Charley loosened his tie and helped him into his chair. Grace listened, spoke quietly, and then hung up the telephone. "Oh, my goodness."

"What is it?" Charley asked in alarm.

"It's Anthony," Lester managed to say between gasps of breath.

"Eleanor is beside herself," Grace said. "Someone's taken the baby."

"Taken? You mean kidnapped?" Charley asked.

"I need to get home." Lester stood unsteadily.

"We need to call the police," Charley said, reaching across the desk for the phone.

"No, not the police! If it's a message to me, they won't want the cops involved."

A message.

Lester was paranoid about messages. He'd originally thought Raymond Palmer's death was a message to him for his west-end development article, but Charley had dispelled that and put forward another theory...in print.

"Do you think this is about the article we ran on the social club raid?" Charley was horrified.

"What else?" He reached for his hat.

"I'll call you a cab," Grace said.

"What do they want?" Charley asked. It couldn't be money. She'd be a much better hostage if that were the case. A retraction? Kidnapping a baby seemed a bit extreme for that. Besides, wouldn't it bring greater attention to the theories she'd hinted at in the story?

"I don't know. I hope—" His voice faltered.

Lester didn't want to involve the police, but Charley knew this was too big for them to handle on their own. "You go home to Eleanor. I have a call to make and then I'll join you. We are going to get Anthony back. I promise."

Charley watched as Lester, leaning heavily on Grace, shuffled out of the newsroom.

She was responsible for this. She had to make things right no matter what it cost her.

He was the last person she wanted to see, but she couldn't think of another option. She picked up the telephone receiver and dialed his number.

An hour later Charley was sitting across from Lester and Eleanor in their small living room. Lester had pulled himself together. Perhaps it was for Eleanor's benefit, but gone was the wretch who'd been slain by a sucker-punch, and in his place was a calm, confident leader in control. For the first time since she'd met him, she could envision Lester as a soldier.

"Can you tell me exactly what happened?" Mark Spadina gently asked Eleanor. He was sitting in Lester's old brown leather chair.

Charley wasn't surprised at Mark's considerate demeanour as he spoke to Eleanor. She'd seen it before, along with other sides to his personality—darker sides that hinted at a man with a complicated past. But since she'd met him seven months ago, Mark had become—well, she didn't quite know what he was at the moment—but he was the first person she called for help. The only person she thought to call.

The ride over had been awkward, at least on her part. Charley hadn't known what to expect when she got into his sedan. After all, she hadn't spoken to the private detective in months—not since their terrible argument when she told him she hated him and never wanted to see him again. But he behaved as if it had never happened. He hadn't even sounded surprised to hear from her and didn't hesitate when she asked for his assistance.

"The baby had been fussy for a few days," Eleanor replied in a voice thick with tears. "Colic. You know how they can be." She glanced up at her husband, who nodded and gave her hand a gentle squeeze.

"Ellie has been under the weather, too," Lester said. "I've tried to spend more time at home, to give her some rest—"

"I understand," Mark said gently. "Go on."

"I had finally gotten him to sleep," Eleanor continued. "I put him down in his crib upstairs and went to the kitchen to make myself a cup of tea. I brought it here and I lay down on the sofa. I was so tired..." Her voice trailed away as she wiped at the tears trailing down her cheek.

"She wasn't asleep for very long. Maybe twenty minutes, isn't that right, Ellie?" Lester said, taking out a handkerchief and passing it to his wife.

She nodded, dabbing at her eyes. "I decided I should go upstairs if I was going to nap. I could get more rest in my own bed. But when I—I—"

"When she went upstairs, she stopped to check on Anthony, but he wasn't there," Lester finished for her.

Eleanor buried her face into Lester's shoulder. Her voice was muffled, but Charley could make out "my fault, my fault."

"And where were you?" Charley asked Emerson, who'd been lurking silently near the entryway since they'd arrived.

"Working," Eleanor's brother said. "I do odd jobs for people in the neighbourhood. I got home at the same time as Les."

Mark scribbled a few lines in his notebook, then closed

it and stood. "We won't keep you any longer. Please don't get up, we'll show ourselves out."

Charley scrambled to her feet. "That's it?"

"For now." He looked down at Lester and Eleanor. "In the meantime, if you hear from the kidnappers, give me a call—no matter what they tell you. I know you don't want to involve the police, but trust me, you don't want to do anything without checking with me first."

"What do you think?" Charley asked once they were back in Mark's car.

"I think we need some food."

"I was talking about the case."

"I know you were, but I think better when my stomach's full and I could hear yours rumbling. When was the last time you ate?"

"My stomach doesn't rumble."

He cocked a dark eyebrow. "No? What does it do? Grumble? Roar? Complain? C'mon, Tiger, admit it. You're starving. Let me buy you dinner and we can discuss the case."

There was no point arguing with him; she *was* hungry. It had been hours since she'd eaten the egg salad sandwich she'd brought from home.

Her stomach truly did rumble the moment the delicious smells of Joe's cooking hit her as they entered the diner. She'd missed coming here, but as much as she loved the food, she knew it was Mark's favourite haunt and she hadn't wanted to risk running into him. Joe waved at them from his station at the grill, behind the long counter, and Gillian handed them menus as they made their way to one of the tables near the back.

Once they'd placed their orders—the fish special for her and liver and onions, with a generous helping of mashed potatoes, for him—she returned to her question about the kidnapping. "So?"

Mark leaned back in his chair and gazed at her with those penetrating dark eyes. "I'm at a bit of a loss, here. It seems a lot has changed since we last spoke."

"What are you talking about?"

"You in cahoots with Pyne. I was gobsmacked when I saw your joint byline last Friday and then again this morning."

"You read the *Trib*?"

"And the *Whig-Standard*. I need to keep up on current events." His eyebrows knit together. "Golly, Tiger, do you think I'm an ignoramus? I can read, you know."

Charley flushed. "Sorry, that's not...I meant...oh, never mind." She took a sip of water. She hated it when he flustered her like this. "Lester has been helping with the new baby."

"So, you're being a good egg and pitching in to help the team."

"Exactly."

"And if you are able to convince John Sherman to put you back on the city beat, that wouldn't be a bad thing, either."

She was saved from having to admit to her ulterior motive by the arrival of their food and they dug in with gusto.

"Do you agree with Pyne that the baby's kidnapping is in response to the article about the raid on the social club?" Mark asked.

"I don't know. I hope not. He didn't write that article. I did."

"I thought I recognized your distinctive style. It was a little too colourful for poor Mr. Pyne."

"Apparently, he subscribes to a new form of journalism, one that discourages any speculation or conjecture."

"And your subtle hinting that the death of a certain city official may not be quite the coincidence it seems is at the heart of it."

Charley felt the fish stirring uncomfortably in her stomach and pushed her plate away. How could she live with herself if she was responsible for baby Anthony's abduction? "Maybe Lester's right and it's better to stick to the dry facts."

"What do you know about this social club? How did you and Pyne get onto that?"

"That wasn't where we started." Charley explained how they'd originally been investigating lobbying efforts by investors to have Kingston annex Township land to support their west-end development proposal and they'd connected Palmer's death, along with Alderman Smythe's, to that story. It was after she learned that Palmer had been the one who had alerted the police to gambling at the Tassisti Social Club that she and Lester had changed their theory about the second death.

"I wouldn't assume the two stories aren't related, especially given Banks' involvement with both," Mark said. "How much do you know about how these gaming syndicates work?"

"Very little. Constable Marillo said I should ask you about them, that you're probably familiar with them from your time as a detective with Toronto PD."

"And I see you rushed right over to get the goods," he said dryly. "No wait. It took the kidnapping of a baby for you to have anything to do with me again."

"Can we stick with the case, please?" If she was honest with herself, she had to admit that a part of her missed him, but there was another part—a large part—that hated the way she always felt he was judging her. She hadn't missed that.

"Sure." He waved to Gillian to bring them more coffee. "Social clubs are often set up by communities or groups with a common interest, and they are incorporated under a provincial charter. What the police have been noticing over the past few years is that gaming syndicates have either been applying for letters patent to incorporate as a social club or buying up charters originally granted to others. On the surface, they look like any other social club—"

"Doing what?" Charley asked.

Mark shrugged. "Whatever the club is designed for. There's a whole whack of them in Toronto. Some are dedicated to athletics—boxing is popular—darts, you name it. Some have political affiliations, some are cultural, others are purely social. There was one we raided that was ostensibly dedicated to playing chess. They can be anything at all. All you need is to get together a group of people with something in common and incorporate yourself as a social club."

"Banks said his tenant was taking over the charter for the Tassisti Social Club."

"Do you know the club's original purpose?"

"I've never heard of it before."

"So, what likely happened is some gamblers discovered a dormant charter and either took it over or bought it and set up a gaming house."

"Can anyone apply for a charter?"

"Sure. As long as the directors on the charter don't have criminal records and the social club pays its taxes, no one's the wiser."

"Why do you think the west-end development deal may be part of it?" Charley asked.

"I don't know for sure if it is. But think about it. The

gambling syndicates are accumulating all this money from illegal betting. What are they going to do with it? They can't deposit it into a bank. Are they going to hide it down a well? No. They need somewhere to stash the cash that looks legit."

"Like Banks buying up half of downtown to hide his diamonds."

"Precisely." Mark leaned forward. "Look, Charley, we're talking about tens of thousands, if not hundreds of thousands of dollars, here. Enough money to kill for. You need to be careful. These guys are the real deal."

"Is this where you give me your usual speech about how you work alone and I'm to stay out of it?"

The intensity of Mark's face broke and a broad smile emerged. "It's never worked before, so I don't imagine you'll listen to me now." He extended his hand. "Welcome to the team, Tiger."

She felt her body grow warm as it did whenever she caught a glimpse of the man beneath the predator. She took his hand and tried to ignore the thrilling tingle as he held it a moment longer than necessary.

Darn it.

THE ELEVATOR DOOR OPENED. Charley stepped out onto the fourth floor of Kingston General Hospital. She'd had another frustrating day at the *Trib*. Understandably, Lester hadn't been in for the past few days and so she'd taken on a few minor stories for the city beat.

The vote on increasing the annexation was supposed to have taken place last evening but had been delayed due to Palmer's death. Apparently, no other staff member was up-to-speed on the proposal and the mayor hadn't wanted to go ahead without someone from the planning department available to respond to questions from elected officials.

Charley had spent the morning interviewing women to take over the advice column for the women's page. She thought it was a ridiculous feature and wanted to drop it, but the advertising department warned there'd be a serious loss of revenue if she did so. In the end, she'd hired sisters Geneva Pecker and Claire Zammit who, between them, had decades of experience counselling young ladies.

The veterans' ward was busier than Charley was used to. She generally visited Laine early in the morning, before heading to the *Tribune*, bringing with her a thermos of decent coffee from home. She hadn't seen her friend for almost a week—not since she'd started helping out on the city beat. Today, though, she'd manage to clear everything urgent off her desk and told Sherman she was leaving early.

She hadn't heard from Mark since their dinner two nights ago. She'd tried calling him several times but he never answered. What kind of private detective didn't have a secretary? Every private eye she'd ever read about or seen in the movies had a Gal Friday to efficiently keep track of his schedule and answer his telephone.

It was exactly a month until Christmas and already decorations were everywhere. On her walk to the hospital, she'd passed a number of shops decked out with the festive adornments of the season, and the city's street crews had started hanging pine boughs and ornaments from the light standards. It reminded her she needed to start thinking of what gifts she'd give to her family and friends. But that would have to wait. She had more pressing matters to deal with first.

Even here, in the hospital, she couldn't escape reminders of the impending season and her lack of preparation for it. Silver stars had been cut out and tacked up outside each of the rooms, and someone had made a paper garland and strung it around the handrail that ran the length of the ward.

She waved and said hello to the nurses and orderlies as she passed them. In a large room, halfway down the hall, several men were playing cards while a few others smoked in quiet camaraderie as they listened to Jack Benny on the radio. She made a point to greet each of the men she passed, even those who stared stonily into the distance, their minds locked away.

Charley heard a deep baritone voice coming from the room Laine had to herself, right beside the nurses' station.

Her friend was sitting by the window, listening intently as Freddie read to her from a large textbook on his lap.

Charley motioned for him to continue as she settled herself on the bed. She didn't understand what he was reading—something to do with pericardial disease, whatever that was. She was impressed, though, with how words such as cytomegalovirus and atherosclerosis slipped easily off his tongue. He closed the book and both he and Laine turned to her.

Anyone meeting Laine in the corridor would never guess she was a patient. She refused to wear a hospital gown and wore her normal day clothes. Today she was wearing khaki pants with a bright orange knit sweater and a colourful scarf. Missing was the lab coat she'd worn as a medical resident.

Charley stared more intently at her brother. His red beard was looking a little scruffy and his clothes were wrinkled as though he'd picked them up off his floor and threw them on. "I didn't expect to see you here," she said to him.

"Freddie comes every day," Laine said, fighting for each word. The bruises from her vicious attack had disappeared long ago. The damage that remained was invisible to the eye. "Stays all day. Late nights, too, sometimes."

"Don't look so surprised," Freddie chided Charley. "Laine gets a headache when she reads so I've been reading her textbooks to her. This way, she won't be so far behind when she's able to return to medical school."

"Dreamer," Laine said smiling fondly at Freddie.

"Do you think you'll be able to finish your medical training? Be a doctor?" Charley asked.

"Not with patients," Laine said. "Maybe research. Long way away, though."

"She remembers everything I read to her. It's all right

here." Freddie tapped his finger against his forehead. "It just takes work to get it from her brain to her tongue. But we'll get there, don't you worry."

"That would be wonderful." It broke her heart to see Laine like this. Her size was diminutive—five-feet at most—but she'd been a huge presence in the emergency room where she'd loved working. If there was any way she could get that back...

"Fifty days," Laine said.

"Fifty days?" Charley glanced between Laine and Freddie. "What does that mean?"

Freddie's pale face flushed pink. "That's how many days I've been sober."

Fifty? Charley hadn't thought he'd gone fifty hours without drinking since he'd returned home from the war. "I'm sorry," she said. "I didn't..." She didn't know what to say. "You haven't been home. I thought..."

"You thought I was out tying one on every night."

"And day. You haven't been around for months."

"I've been either here or at my classes on campus."

"Is it because of Evelyn and your impending Earldom or whatever it's called? Is that why you've stopped?"

Freddie shook his head. "No, I've known about that for years." He gazed fondly at Laine. "It's because of her. She refused to see me if I wasn't completely sober. At first, I'd skip drinking the night before I came to visit, and then I started visiting every day, so I stopped altogether."

"Program," Laine said.

"Yes, and at Laine's insistence, I joined that new abstinence program everyone is talking about. There's a group of us, mostly former soldiers, who meet here every day."

"I am so pleased," Charley said.

"Relieved, I bet," he said.

"Yes, that too. But you know, it's not fair to Gran to have to take care of Evelyn all the time—not when you invited her here."

Freddie's attention turned to removing a spot on the cover of the textbook.

"Are you going to go back with her?" Charley finally asked the question that had been preying on her since Evelyn's unexpected arrival two months ago.

"I don't know. I haven't decided yet."

"But this earl thing didn't come as a surprise to you, did it? You visited her after the war, during those months we thought you were dead." She saw him blanch at the accusation. He had no idea how she and Gran had suffered. They'd hidden their pain because he'd been so fragile since his return. But now things were coming to a head. Evelyn had arrived with the clear intention of taking Freddie back to the Midlands with her.

"I am sorry about that," he said in a hushed tone.

"Can you tell me what happened? How you ended up in England? Did you find her or did she find you?"

Freddie held up his hands to ward off more questions. "I'll tell you everything." He took a deep breath and then gave Laine a rueful grin. "And then I'll need a meeting."

"You are stronger than you think," Laine said.

Freddie gave her a grateful smile and then turned to Charley. "After Dieppe, I was taken prisoner by the Jerries. We got moved around a lot. A few months here, a year there. It all depended on what type of labour they needed— mining, logging, farming." His voice was a monotone, as if he was reciting a script. Maybe he needed to do it this way —remove as much of the emotion as he could from the memory.

"By January of '45, it was obvious the war was going

badly for Germany," he continued. "We were taken out of the camps and forced to march all over the country. It was cold. We slept on the ground and foraged for food in ditches and barnyards. Some of the guards deserted and disappeared into the night. The ones who stayed turned even more brutal. About four months later...four months?" He cocked his head and paused. "Yes, I guess that's right. Anyway, we were met by advancing Soviet troops who drove the Germans out. In a way, we were saved. But we still needed to make it back to England and by the time we did, those of us who were still alive were in pretty desperate shape."

Charley squeezed her eyes closed to hold back the tears. Freddie's matter-of-fact description was so much worse than what she'd imagined. It was no wonder he'd sought oblivion in a bottle.

"I've known about Evelyn for years," Freddie said, his voice returning to normal. "Grandpa told me about the Pierreponts when I turned sixteen."

"Did Gran know this?"

"Oh, I doubt it. He said I had a right to know that I was the sole heir to the title and, at some point, I'd have to decide what to do about it."

"You never said anything about it to me."

"Honestly, I didn't think much about it at all. I couldn't imagine leaving Kingston, ever. But then I found myself in England and I couldn't imagine going home again—not after..." He paused and swallowed heavily. "She arranged for me to be brought to the Midlands and to be cared for by the best doctors and nurses. Eventually, I recovered and told her I wanted to go home."

"I bet she wasn't happy about that."

"You judge her too harshly. She has no one, you know.

She's lonely. She didn't want me to leave, but she didn't stop me, either."

Charley gazed past Freddie to look out the window. Clouds were gathering and she wondered if it would snow. With Christmas a month away, it would be nice if there was snow.

"More," Laine said.

"I don't need to hear anything more," Charley said. "I'm so sorry for what you went through, Freddie."

"Tell her," Laine insisted.

"Okay, okay." Freddie took a deep shuddering breath. "Part of the program is to make restitution to those I've harmed and—"

"Hey ho, who planned the party and forgot to send me an invitation?" Mark sauntered into the room. "Hey, Doc." He gently touched Laine on the shoulder. "Cap'n." He shook Freddie's hand and then sat down on the bed beside Charley. "Grace told me you'd be here."

Charley was relieved by the interruption. She wasn't sure what Freddie had been going to tell her—no, that wasn't true. She was afraid she did know what he'd been going to tell her. *Theo.* Up until that moment, that was the one thing she'd wanted from him more than anything. To know what happened to her husband. But after listening to his harrowing story of surviving the German POW camps, she wasn't sure she could take any more right now.

"How's the studying going?" Mark asked.

"You know about that?" Charley asked.

"Sure, the detective stops by quite often," Freddie replied.

"I feel like I'm completely out to lunch," Charley said.

Laine shook her head. She pointed her finger at

Charley: "Morning." Pointed at Freddie: "Afternoon." And then at Mark: "Evening."

"And when does poor Grace get to see you?" Charley asked.

"Night." Laine grinned.

"I hate to break up this party, but I need to talk to you, Tiger." Mark stood up.

"Okay, I'll let you get back to your medical textbook," Charley said.

"Nope," Freddie said, putting the textbook under his chair. "We alternate. A chapter of gory medical gobbledy-gook and a chapter of scintillating prose or poetry." He held up a much smaller book. "You'll like this one, Detective."

"*The Woman in White*," Mark said, reading the cover.

"By Wilkie Collins. It was written in 1859 and is considered to be one of the first mystery novels ever written. A pioneer of what's known as sensation novels." He wiggled his eyebrows suggestively.

"Oh well, you need to let your grandmother know about that one," Mark quipped. "She could use a diversion from the cases of Miss Marple, and a 'sensation' novel sounds like the perfect choice for her book club."

"Oh brother," Charley rolled her eyes. For some reason, Mark had taken an inordinate interest in Gran's reading habits and it irked her more than it should. She grabbed his arm and pulled him toward the door. "Let's go."

She waited in front of the hospital for Mark to retrieve his car. "Do you have any news?" she asked, sliding into the passenger seat.

"I've been in contact with some old pals in Toronto and they put me in touch with Sergeant Anderson of the provincial police's anti-gambling branch. He's been assigned to this area." He signalled and pulled away from the curb. "I asked him about the original charter for the Tassisti Social Club. Do you know what Tassisti means?"

She shook her head.

"It's Italian for taxi drivers. The original charter was set up to benefit the drivers of Kingston's original taxi co-operative."

"I didn't know Kingston had a taxi co-operative," she said.

"It doesn't anymore, and the charter for the club's been dormant for years. But guess who the founding president was?"

She hated it when he toyed with her like this. "How would I know?"

"A Mister Romeo Arcadi."

"Romeo Arcadi?" Charley whispered under her breath.

"I don't know why you're so surprised," Mark said.

"That he is capable of kidnapping a baby and killing two men? Of course I'm surprised. He seems like—"

"'Such a nice man.' I know, that's what you keep saying. But who knows what evil lurks in the hearts of men?" He chuckled and added in a dramatic voice: "The Shadow knows!"

Charley scowled at him. "I think you're as enamored with detective stories as Gran and her book club ladies."

They'd been sitting across the street from the taxi depot for forty minutes. Mark called it a stake-out. He wanted to make sure their suspect was there and to see how many other drivers were present before they confronted Arcadi. There were typically two or three men standing outside the entrance, their cigarette smoke blended with the frosty air, cloaking them in a misty veil. Every once in awhile Arcadi would come out of the building to hand one of them a piece of paper. The driver would grind the cigarette under his shoe and leave. There were a lot of comings and goings among the cabbies, but not for Arcadi.

The sun was dipping lower on the horizon. It would be dark in less than an hour.

"It's getting late. Wouldn't it be better to come back tomorrow? Talk to him in the daytime? Or maybe go to his home? I'm sure Grace has found out where he lives by now." Charley had called Grace from a corner pay phone as soon as Mark told her about Arcadi's name being on the original charter. "Do we need to accuse him in his place of business?"

"We're not going to accuse him of anything. We're going to ask him a few questions. I can't believe you're the one urging caution. Lester Pyne has had an undue influence on you, and I don't like it one bit."

"That's not true," Charley said. "But I would feel better if we knew more about him."

"What is it about this that has you so rattled?" Mark angled toward her.

She was rattled. For the past six months Arcadi had been driving her all over town, almost as a personal chauffeur, and yet she didn't know why. She'd even stopped wondering about it, accepting that when she requested a cab, he'd arrive and refuse to take any money. Sometimes he'd show up without her calling, almost as if he knew she'd be needing him and his taxi.

"Is it because he saved your life that time?" Mark asked.

Yes, there's that, too.

"Let's check with Grace and do this tomorrow," she said.

"No can do, Tiger. Every hour we wait is an hour the Pyne's baby is in jeopardy." The last of the cabbies got into his vehicle and pulled out onto the street. "Arcadi's alone. Let's go."

"Did you know they'd all be gone at some point?" She followed him out of the car and across the road.

"I had a hunch. It's the end of the workday and people

are anxious to get home to their dinners. It's bound to be the busiest time."

Romeo Arcadi didn't look up from his desk when they entered his office, which was situated just to the right of the small entryway to the building. He held up his hand for them to remain quiet and continued totalling up his ledger.

Charley took the time to glance around his office. No sign of an infant, but then she'd hardly expect him to bring the baby to work with him. Too many questions.

When Arcadi finally looked up, he dropped his pencil and leapt to his feet. "Mrs. Hall. Detective Spadina. This is a surprise. What are you doing here?"

"We'd like to talk to you about the Tassisti Social Club," Mark said.

Arcadi's brow furrowed and he cocked his head to the side. "Tassisti?" He sank back into his chair. "Sit, please." He motioned with his hand for them to do the same. "I haven't thought about Tassisti in years."

"Didn't you see it in the newspaper this week?" Charley asked, suspiciously. "It was on the front page of both the *Trib* and *Whig-Standard*."

He shrugged. "I'm sorry, but this has been an unbelievably bad week for me. My dispatcher quit and several of my drivers have been sick. Why was Tassisti in the newspaper?"

"The club was raided by the police over the weekend and they arrested a number of men for gambling."

"Gambling?" Arcadi tsked. "Why are you coming to me about this? It cannot be the same Tassisti. We would play cards and darts, certainly. Sometimes the drivers would even make small wagers on the outcome. But I don't think this is what you are talking about, is it Detective?"

"No, Mr. Arcadi, it's not," Mark replied. "These

gamblers are professional criminals who are operating gaming houses and betting syndicates. And the money involved is quite a bit greater than a wager among friends."

"And, again, I must ask, what involvement in this do you think I have?"

"Tassisti," Mark said. "You are listed as president on the original charter of incorporation."

"Yes, but it cannot be the same one. You must be mistaken."

"Why do you say that?" Charley asked.

"When we originally set it up, it was to provide the taxi drivers with a place to talk and relax from the day."

"You were a co-operative then, correct?" Charley asked.

"Yes, at that time. But then the war came and having a place like Tassisti seemed wrong when so many of our brothers were fighting overseas."

"So, the charter became dormant," Mark said.

"Yes. Dormant. The rules say if you are not active for five years, you become dormant. I made this official with the province in 1944. Tassisti was finished."

"Why wouldn't you just wait and resume activities once the war ended?" Charley asked.

"Many things had changed. We were no longer a co-operative."

"Someone bought you out?" she asked.

Arcadi glanced down at his ledger.

"No, wait," Charley said. "*You* bought them out. This is your taxi company." Why hadn't she realized this before? It made no sense that an employee would refuse money for a fare, but an owner...

He looked up. "It is, yes."

"And am I the only customer you drive personally?"

His smile creased the corners of his eyes. "And your grandmother."

"Why?"

He shrugged. "It does not matter. It simply is."

"What does that mean?" A ripple of unease coursed through her.

"Let's get back to Tassisti, shall we?" Mark interjected.

Charley had many more questions, but they'd have to wait. "Fine."

"The charter was never cancelled," Mark said.

"How can that be?"

"You need to file a final tax return," Mark said. "If you don't, the government keeps the charter open."

"My partner, the treasurer, he was to do it."

"Well, according to my sources, he didn't."

"So, someone stole Tassisti's name to set up this gambling den?" Arcadi looked indignant.

"It's not quite that simple. These gambling syndicates try to hide under legitimate businesses. They would have had to apply to the government to formally take over the charter with a new slate of directors and file annual tax returns—including those for the years it was dormant," Mark explained.

Arcadi rocketed to his feet. "We'll go see Paulie now."

"Paulie is the treasurer?" Charley guessed.

"Paul Bigelow, yes. He and I started the co-operative, but he..." Arcadi's hands flailed as if they could pluck from air the words he was searching for. "Come. You will see."

***

CHARLEY SAT on a threadbare sofa in a chilly, gloomy sitting room of a rooming house in a less than reputable neighbourhood of the city. Only a purple crocheted afghan, draped across the back of one of the chairs, provided any colour to the drab room. She was squeezed between Mark and Arcadi as they waited for the housemother to fetch Paul Bigelow.

She glanced through the doorway to the dining room where three burly men were playing cards. They looked rough, like the area, and she was glad Mark was with her.

She appreciated Mark's desire to focus on the case—baby Anthony was the priority, of course—but she couldn't help wondering why Arcadi had taken such an interest in her. Had he appointed himself her personal driver so he could keep tabs on her and her work for the *Trib*? Mark had dismissed that theory when she shared it with him on the drive to the rooming house. He'd pointed out that Arcadi had appeared at the time she'd been moved off the city beat and placed on the women's pages. It was hardly the type of reporting someone involved in criminal activities was likely to care about. He had a point. Lester, with his focus on the city's policies and policing, would be a far better mark.

Then again, Arcadi had been more inquisitive than usual the last time he'd driven her—and that had been right after she and Lester had confronted Colin Banks who had his own connection to the Tassisti Social Club.

Preceded by the sound of grinding metal, the house-mother appeared pushing a wheelchair. Arcadi and Mark rose to their feet and stayed standing as she positioned it in a space between two chairs that sat across from the sofa. "I'll leave you to it. Don't be too long, mind. His dinner's in a half-hour and I don't wait."

As Arcadi made introductions, Charley examined Paul Bigelow. Despite the two painfully skinny legs outlined under a pair of too-loose trousers, it was obvious he'd once been a tall, physical man. His shoulders were still broad; however, his arms and hands were covered by a beige woolen blanket that had been wrapped around him. She glanced over at the empty hearth. A fire would go a long way to improving both the temperature and bleakness of the room.

While Bigelow's lower and upper body remained immobile, his head seemed to exist in a separate reality, and he turned to each of them as they were introduced. He couldn't shake their hands, but his clear blue eyes and engaging smile made Charley feel as if she'd been greeted warmly.

"I am so pleased to meet you." His voice, however, was weak and reedy. "I so rarely get to meet anyone new." He coughed several times, an unhealthy bark.

Arcadi jumped up, pounded his back and adjusted the blanket.

"Thank you, my friend," Bigelow said.

"You need to see the doctor again. That cough isn't getting any better," Arcadi scolded.

"The doctor will tell me what he always does: there is nothing to be done. And then he will charge me an exorbitant amount of money for the privilege of his company," Bigelow said, fighting back another coughing attack.

"Let me get to the point of our visit then," Arcadi said. "It's about Tassisti. Criminals have taken our charter and are using it to run a gambling den."

"It can't be. You terminated the charter years ago," Bigelow said.

"The final tax return was never filed," Mark said. "Until that happens, the charter is merely dormant."

"I am so sorry, Romeo. The fault is all mine." Bigelow lowered his head. "I intended to file it, but..." He raised his gaze to Charley, and she could see his despair. "My car was hit by a truck and, well, as you can see, I fared no better than my poor taxi." He turned to Arcadi. "I completely forgot and now our precious Tassisti has been taken over by criminals. What a legacy to leave." His body convulsed as he was wracked by another coughing fit.

"It is all right, Paulie," Arcadi said as he pounded on the man's back again. "I will see that it is made right." He glanced over to Charley and Mark.

Mark nodded, satisfied with the explanation.

"We'll leave so you can have your meal." Arcadi straightened. "Allow me to push you into the dining room."

"Well, so much for that," Charley whispered to Mark. "Neither Arcadi nor Bigelow look like they're rolling in dough—at least not the type of money you say these gamblers make."

"Don't be so sure. Are you familiar with the expression sometimes you can't see the wood for the trees?"

"Of course."

"Then ask yourself this: after years in a financial depression and with the country at war, how is Arcadi able to buy out all the other taxi drivers in his co-op?"

Charley peered into the dining room before entering.

"Don't slink around like a thief in the night. Come in," Bessie snapped at her.

"Sorry, Gran. I'm making sure the coast is clear." Charley bent to kiss the older woman's cheek before taking her seat at the table and pouring herself a cup of coffee from the urn. She thanked Rachel, who'd appeared at her side to scoop out a serving of scrambled eggs and ham from the gold-trimmed Limoges platter.

"You needn't worry. I've been eating breakfast alone all week because you are on your way as soon as the sun is up, and Evelyn, it seems, has the same morning habit as your brother and doesn't make an appearance until almost noon."

"It's quite common in England for the upper classes to lie in until late morning," Rachel said.

"Is that what she's doing?" Bessie asked, her voice tinged with sarcasm.

"Yes, ma'am. I generally bring her tea—"

"In bed?" The incredulity in Bessie's voice rose it an octave. "You've been serving her tea in bed every morning?"

Rachel's breath caught and her face turned a fiery red. "Yes, ma'am."

"Well, it stops immediately. In this house, breakfast is served in the dining room. I don't care if she is a countess, she can darn well get up out of bed and join us lesser mortals down here."

"But—" Rachel began.

It was the first time Charley had ever seen the house-keeper flustered. She almost felt sorry for her.

Rachel lowered her head and murmured, "Yes, ma'am," before scurrying out of the room.

"Well that cinches it," Charley said. "She's got to be a spy for Evelyn."

"Of course she is."

"Then why do you let her stay?"

"She's the best housekeeper we've had in years." Bessie took a sip of her coffee. "Besides, I don't believe it's you or me that Evelyn is looking for intelligence on."

Freddie.

"You're probably right, but I do wish you'd waited until I was back at work on Monday before you started forcing Evelyn to come down to breakfast."

Charley took a forkful of eggs, her thoughts returning to baby Anthony. Lester hadn't heard anything from the kidnappers, which surprised her. She hadn't heard anything from Mark, which didn't.

Can't see the wood for the trees.

Grace had found nothing incriminating on Romeo Arcadi. He'd come to Canada from Italy after the Great War, married and had four children—two boys, two girls. Three were married with families of their own. Arcadi's wife died a year ago. He still lived in the home he'd purchased in 1921. Arcadi was listed as the founding president of the taxi co-operative, and then as its owner after purchasing the shares of the other driver-members.

Paul Bigelow was born in Hamilton and had moved to Kingston when he was in his twenties. He'd been treasurer of the co-operative since its formation and sold his share to Arcadi in 1939, continuing to work as a taxi driver for Arcadi, like most of the others. Grace had found an article from the *Hamilton Spectator* that mentioned the accident that had paralyzed him in 1945. About the only interesting thing about Bigelow was that he'd lived in that dreary boarding house they'd visited for almost twenty years. Charley had assumed he'd been forced to move there when he could no longer work.

Can't see the wood for the trees.

"I don't want you using Mr. Arcadi's taxi anymore," Charley said.

"Why on earth not?" Bessie lowered the knife she'd been using to butter her toast.

"He might be involved in something..." Charley shrugged. "I don't know for sure, but don't you think it's strange that he is the one who always comes when we call for a cab? And that he won't take any payment?"

Bessie took a bite of her toast and chewed it thoughtfully. "Romeo Arcadi is a perfectly respectable business operator," she said finally. "If he chooses not to demand payment for his services, that's his prerogative. It's certainly not because he doesn't think we can afford it."

"That's what I mean. Why would he do that?"

"I am afraid the nature of your job has made you overly suspicious. You are looking for trouble where there is none."

"But—"

"Enough, Charlotte. I won't listen to you make unsubstantiated accusations against people simply because they act in a manner you do not understand."

Charley slumped back against her chair. Why wouldn't

Gran trust her instincts? She may not have definitive proof, but there were certainly enough signs to raise some troubling doubts.

"Don't pout," Bessie chided.

"I'm not pouting. It's just..."

"Go on."

Charley pushed her plate away. "You don't take any of my concerns seriously. Not about Romeo Arcadi. Not about Rachel Winters. And not about Evelyn."

Bessie's eyes widened. "What about Evelyn?"

"That it was Freddie she wanted when we were children."

"It didn't matt—"

"Yes, I know: It didn't matter because you wouldn't let her take either of us anyway." Charley said, uncharacteristically interrupting her grandmother. "But it matters to me."

"You are making this far too personal."

"Of course it's personal. My own grandmother didn't want me."

Bessie's face softened with compassion. "You misunderstand. She didn't want Freddie, either. She wanted an heir. It made no difference who or what it was so long as it could inherit the title. Good heavens, if she could have made do with a teacup she would have."

Charley snorted at the image.

"I wouldn't give Evelyn Pierrepont another thought. Well, except to decide what you intend to give her as a present for Christmas, of course."

"A present? For Evelyn?" Charley gaped at her grandmother. She had barely started to think about what gifts she'd get for her family and friends. A present for her maternal grandmother hadn't even entered into her consideration.

"Charlotte, you must get her something."

"Maybe I'll get her a teacup."

Gran chuckled. "That's a marvelous idea. But in all seriousness, you shouldn't fret about Evelyn and whatever her agenda is. She's Freddie's problem."

"Maybe so, but it is galling that it's the fact that he's male that makes him so valuable."

"He is the elder of the two of you."

"If he'd been a girl, Evelyn would be out of luck," Charley insisted. "It's the same at work. Men get all the advantages."

"You are still employed. Most people would see the move from reporter to editor as a promotion," Bessie said.

"I wasn't given the choice."

"If you genuinely want to help your sex, the women's page is exactly where you need to be. It's there you have the ability and authority to elevate the voices of women in this community."

"In amongst the fluffy stories about fashion and fundraisers."

Bessie chuckled. "We make gains where we can."

"Is this what you envisioned when you marched for women to have the right to vote? Charley asked. "You went to jail for it. And now—"

"And now I seem content to host fundraisers and go to book club with my suffragette sisters?"

"Well, yes. Sorry, Gran, I don't mean to sound disrespectful. I don't understand why you force me to conform when you didn't."

"To get the vote, we needed the men in power to give it to us. First, we had to get their attention, and then we had to get their permission. We couldn't be subtle."

"But securing the vote for women can't be the end of it.

We are a long way from being equal. I have to be twice as good to get half the advantages of any of the male reporters at the *Tribune*."

"I didn't leave my family to march in the streets and spend a night in jail to have us all turn into men." Bessie's expression was fierce. "Heavens to Betsy, we just fought two great wars that were brought about by the vanity of that sex. No, if society is going to thrive, women must be allowed to be women." Her features softened. "You, my darling Charlotte, have so much passion for what you do. Wear trousers if you must, but don't succumb to the temptation to behave as men do. You truly do your best work and can raise us all —women and men—when you are yourself." Bessie reached across the table and squeezed Charley's hand. "And now you'll want to excuse yourself. I believe I hear Evelyn coming down the stairs."

Charley pushed back her chair, kissed Gran, and made a hasty exit. She greeted Evelyn with a stilted "good morning" as they passed in the hallway.

In the drawing room, she settled down with the weekend issue of the *Trib* but her focus kept migrating from the newspaper to her conversation with Bessie. Gran didn't get it. The last time she'd written a major article for the *Tribune* as "herself," she'd put a baby's life in jeopardy. Lester had intoned time and again that journalism was changing; if she wanted to make her mark she was going to have to change, too.

By winning the vote for women, Gran and her contemporaries had succeeded in taking the first step toward an equal society. Now, it was up to her generation to continue the journey. Charley was under no illusions that it would be any easier for them.

She'd made it to page three when she heard Rachel enter the room to announce, "Alderman Cannon is here to see you."

Dan's here?

"Show him in, please." Charley was surprised to hear the quiver in her voice. "And bring some coffee, if you would?"

"Of course, Mrs. Hall." The housekeeper wouldn't meet her gaze.

Charley took a deep breath to settle her nerves. She folded the newspaper and set it on the side table. A jolt of apprehension surged through her as she rose to her feet. What was going on? She'd never been nervous around Dan before. But then, she'd never seen him as angry as he was the last time they'd been together.

"Charley." He said her name without any animosity as he entered the room. He wore his Saturday casual clothes: blue trousers and a light blue and red knit sweater over a white crew-neck tee-shirt.

She ran her hands down the skirt of the belted plaid dress she was wearing—the feminine attire she adopted for Gran's benefit most weekends. "I'm surprised to see you."

He ran his hand through his hair and gave her a sheepish smile. Her heart flip-flopped at the familiar gesture.

"We didn't part very well, did we?" he said. "I am sorry about that."

Her legs felt weak with relief—he didn't hate her—and she sank into her chair. "Sit, please. Rachel's going to bring us some coffee."

He nodded and took the chair beside hers.

"I didn't mean to upset you, and I'm not trying to break up your engagement with Meredith," Charley said. "But—"

"No." He held up his hand. "I don't want to hear it. You're going to tell me that Meredith isn't her real name. It's Merisse. I know that. I realize you think you're trying to protect me, but you don't need to."

"What about your plan to run for Parliament?"

"What about it?"

"The scandal…" Was he suddenly so much in love with Meredith Banks that he was prepared to be willfully blind to what the evidence showed? Her brother was a Nazi collaborator and maybe worse if that was possible. Any association with him would ruin Dan.

"All you have is a bunch of half-baked theories about Colin's time in Europe. You have to trust me on this, Charley. There is no scandal. No story. Please, let it go."

"I can't promise you that."

"Well, can you at least promise you'll talk to me *before* you publish anything?" He leaned forward. "If I ever meant anything to you, please do this for me."

He'd once meant the world to her and she'd have gone to the ends of the earth to protect him. If he refused to see the truth, she wasn't sure she could help him, but she could at least honour this request. "Okay."

He craned his neck and angled his head towards her, trying to look behind her back.

"What are you doing?"

"Making sure you haven't crossed your fingers. It wouldn't be the first time I was duped." His wink took the sting out of the accusation.

She held up her hands and wiggled her fingers in front of his face. "Not crossed, as you can see."

"Thank you." He leaned back. "In return, I may have a piece of information that will interest you."

Charley waited as Rachel carried in a tray with two steaming cups of coffee. The housekeeper handed one to Charley and asked Dan if he'd like cream or sugar in his. He declined both.

"When did you start drinking your coffee black?" Charley asked once they were alone.

"Since I've become too busy to do my regular physical fitness regime. I've noticed my trousers are starting to feel tight."

Charley snorted. "I thought it was women who were supposed to be vain."

"It's not vanity. It's my public image."

"Hmmm." Charley took a sip of her coffee. "Most politicians I know are round, bald, and smoke cigars."

"That's *after* they get elected."

Charley figured Dan's concern about his weight had less to do with his political future and more about his impending marriage. That was a topic she'd rather avoid, so she asked, "What is this information you have for me?"

"This is deep background. Off the record."

"Deep background? Now I'm intrigued."

"Off the record," he insisted.

She nodded and wiggled her fingers at him as proof.

"Okay. So, you know Raymond Palmer was responsible

for organizing the city's response to the proposal to annex the land around Gardiners Road, right?"

She nodded. "The vote was supposed to be last week, but it was delayed."

"Yes. The mayor wanted time to allow someone else from the planning department to be familiar with the file in case we had any questions before the council had to vote on it."

"Okay?" Charley wondered why Dan's cheeks had coloured and he seemed breathless.

"So, the fellow that got the nod is a fairly new staffer. I guess the mayor thought since all the work had been done by Palmer, Vincent would only need to read through the file, which he did."

"You are taking a long road to get to the point."

"He brought the full file to me because he had some questions."

"Why would he bring it to you and not Carruthers? He's the alderman for the area."

Dan stared down at his hands. "As I said, he's fairly new and...oh, heck. He's the son of one of my supporters. I got him the job." He stood and fished in one of his front pockets, pulling out a page that had been folded into a square. "He showed me this. He didn't know what it meant or why it was in the file." Dan sat down but held onto the paper. "I remembered the article you and Pyne wrote that mentioned the sale of a hotel. I thought it was odd that it was lumped into a story about the west-end development. A private sale of a hotel isn't something city council concerns itself with. But then Vincent showed me this."

Charley extended her hand.

"Did Palmer talk to you about the hotel? Is that why it was in the article?" Dan handed her the page.

"I didn't talk to Palmer, Pyne did." Charley unfolded the page. She immediately recognized the letterhead of a local bank. The copy was grainy but readable. The branch manager was writing to the current hotel owner to assure him that his client had the funds needed to provide his forty-nine per cent share for the purchase of the hotel.

Pretty routine.

But then she saw it. The client was Ronald P. Adams, a constable with the Kingston Police Department.

———

CONSTABLE ADAMS.

Charley had never liked the guy, but she hadn't thought he was dirty. Crooked cops were something she thought were made up by the authors of pulp fiction.

She paced her bedroom.

How could Adams afford to buy a hotel—even half a hotel—on a cop's salary? Dan had told her how much constables make. It would take years for Adams to save enough money, and he hadn't been with the police department nearly that long. Plus, Adams was always short of cash. How many times had she seen him ask Marillo to spot him some coin?

The letter looked legitimate. She scribbled *"visit bank"* on her notepad right underneath where she'd written "have Grace check out Adams." She knew the bank manager wouldn't willingly discuss a client, but she was confident she'd be able to get something out of him if she mentioned the letter. Too bad Dan didn't allow her to keep it. He said he needed to return it to the file.

Why was it in that file to begin with? Was it a coincidence or did Palmer think it was related to the west-end development? If Adams thought that Lester got the information about the hotel from Palmer, he'd probably worry about whether Palmer knew he was one of the buyers.

Her breath caught. Maybe she and Lester had been right the first time and Palmer's death wasn't due to the police raid on the Tassisti Social Club but rather the original article Lester had written, which mentioned the hotel as well as the proposed development. Adams had been angry with him that Friday morning: "You've opened a real can of worms," she'd heard him say. Lester had downplayed the argument, claiming Adams was merely upset at the way police were portrayed in newspapers. But what if it wasn't about that? Why would Lester lie about it?

Was Adams being bought off for killing Smythe? Was he guilty of murder or simply lying about the cause of death? Had he killed Palmer, too? Marillo said his partner had volunteered to work those weekends—alone.

She wrote *"Talk to Marillo again."*

Why buy him a hotel? Why not just give Adams the money?

Mark had suggested the Gardiners Road development could be a means for the Tassisti gambling syndicate to stash its earnings somewhere that looked legitimate. Wouldn't a hotel do the same for Adams? Heck, they could even run a betting house out of it.

A chill raced down her spine. It was all related. Gardiners Road. The Tassisti Social Club. The hotel. Smythe. Palmer. Baby Anthony.

Oh, my goodness, Lester, what have we gotten ourselves into?

She picked up the phone and arranged for Mark to meet her at Lester's home.

"I HATE DIRTY COPS," Mark muttered after Charley had filled him and Lester in on her conversation with Dan and her speculation about what that letter meant. "It takes one to give us all a bad name."

Charley refrained from commenting that he was no longer a cop and that he'd been fired from the Toronto Police Department for breaking its rules. It wasn't the same, she knew. Mark hadn't taken any bribes. He'd gone AWOL and pretended to be in Kingston on behalf of the Toronto force when he'd actually been conducting a personal investigation into his mother's death. Apparently, you could be guilty of impersonating a police officer even when you were one.

"I don't believe it," Lester said, shaking his head.

"How else could he afford a hotel if he wasn't on the take?" Charley said.

"No, I don't buy it. Not Adams," Lester insisted.

"I've seen it before," Mark said. "It's how these syndicates operate."

Why was Lester being so dogmatic about Adams' innocence? "Why not Adams?" she challenged him. "You brushed off the argument I saw you having with him. What do you know that we don't?"

Lester's eyes darted back and forth between Mark and Charley like a trapped rabbit. "You're right, he unhappy about the article. Said I'd revealed too much but wouldn't say what part." Then he leaned forward and lowered his voice. "This can't leave the room: Adams is my contact in the police department. He was the one who told me to look deeper into Alderman Smythe's death. If he was involved, why would he risk being implicated?"

"If there were suspicions about Smythe's cause of death, a good cop wouldn't have filed it as an accident," Mark said.

Exactly!

"I am so glad you could come. I apologize for the late invitation." Meredith Banks beamed at Charley.

The invitation to Sunday brunch had been waiting when she'd returned from meeting with Mark and Lester. Her first thought had been to refuse—she wasn't sure she wanted to socialize with Dan's *fiancée*—but then her reporter's instincts kicked in and she wondered if she'd be able to find out more about Banks from his sister. She felt a twinge of guilt at using Meredith but reminded herself that whether or not the woman was involved in her brother's treason, she almost certainly knew about it given she'd changed her name, too.

Besides, it got her out of having to face Evelyn at breakfast.

"I appreciate you sending a car," Charley said stepping into the grand foyer.

"Oh, it was nothing. I am just so pleased you are here."

Charley was relieved when Mrs. Harper arrived to take her coat and hat. She'd been fearful that history would repeat itself and she'd be alone with her hostess. She shook off the ghosts of the past, reminding herself that it was Meredith who had saved her that day.

"Is your brother going to join us?" Charley asked.

"No. He and Dan are having their own *tête-à-tête* downtown. It will be the two of us." Concern clouded her light grey eyes. "I hope that's okay."

"Of course."

Meredith was pale, fine-boned and slim. She moved with an elegant grace that made Charley feel like a lumbering oaf as she followed her down the hallway. Before reaching the kitchen, they veered off into the lovely glassed-in breakfast nook that overlooked the gardens. The flowers were gone for the season, but the yew bushes surrounding the perimeter had kept their greenery. Charley shivered as the ghosts returned. Since Adeline Banks' poisonings of Kingston's nurses last summer, she would never be able to look at a yew bush in quite the same way again.

"Oh, goodness. I never thought..." Meredith's hand flew to her mouth. "We can go to the dining room."

Charley was impressed. Meredith couldn't be more than twenty and yet she possessed the perception and poise of someone more mature in years. She'd make an excellent politician's wife. "No, this is a lovely room. Let's enjoy the sunshine." Charley sat down in the chair with its back to the garden.

"Coffee, black?" Meredith asked.

"Yes, thank you." Charley accepted the steaming cup and took a sip. "Delicious."

Of course.

"We import it from South Africa. Colin is very fussy about his coffee. Dan says you are, too, so I'm glad you like it."

"Do you miss South Africa?" Charley asked, surprised at how easily Meredith had made it for her to broach the subject.

"No. I miss some of my friends, of course, but I don't

miss the politics of the place." She waited while a young woman placed bowls of soup in front of them. A second woman put a platter of assorted slices of bread, cheeses, and fruits in the centre of the table. "I hope pea soup is to your liking. It's been frightfully cold lately and this house doesn't keep its heat very well."

"It all looks wonderful." Charley reached for a slice of thick, pumpernickel bread and slathered it with butter. "What was it about the politics you didn't like? You were quite young when you left for boarding school, weren't you?"

"Twelve."

"And already you were uncomfortable with the country's politics?" Charley asked.

"Not so much the country's politics. But certainly my father's."

"He was a member of the *Ossewabrandwag*. His loyalty during the war was with Germany."

Charley feared she'd gone too far too quickly as Meredith lowered her spoon, cocked her head to the side, and gazed at her quizzically. Suddenly the young woman's face erupted into an enormous grin. "Dan said you were dogged."

Charley felt off-balance by Meredith's response. "I didn't mean to be forward. Gran always criticizes me for being nosy."

"I feel you and I have come here with a common purpose," Meredith said. "You were hoping to get intelligence about my brother's activities during the war and I was wanting to tell you about them."

"You were?" She may have felt off-balance before but now she was totally floored. Did Meredith intend to turn her brother in?

She nodded. "Very few people know the truth. Dan is one of them."

"How long has he known?"

"Colin told him the basics when they first met. I think he left out a few details, which surprised Dan when you and Mr. Pyne were here last week."

"That you and your brother changed your names."

Meredith nodded. "Yes, but that was all." Meredith leaned forward. "My brother is a very honourable man and wouldn't have felt comfortable offering his support to Dan without first telling him about what he did during the war and how we came to Canada."

"And Dan agreed to take his support anyway?"

"Do you think he only learned the truth after our engagement was announced? That he is so much in love with me that nothing else mattered?" Meredith tsked. "You, of all people, know better than that. When he proposed to me, Dan was still in love with you."

Charley fell back in her chair and stared at the woman "If you believe that, why did you accept his proposal?"

"I am in love with him. We are a good match and I truly believe that in time, he will come to love me. Besides, you don't have the disposition to be a politician's wife, do you?" The last statement was said without malice.

"I've heard that a lot," Charley admitted. "For what it's worth, I do think he's falling in love with you."

"I hope so. I know he respects me, and that's a very good start for a marriage, I think."

Charley stared into her empty soup bowl. She wished she could dislike Meredith Banks, but every encounter they'd had left her more and more impressed by the young woman. "You don't have to tell me whatever your family's secret is," she said, raising her gaze. "I'll stop pressing Dan about your brother."

"Unfortunately, that's not going to work. I don't want Dan to have to keep secrets from you. It is too hard on him and one day he may come to resent us—Colin and me —for it."

The conversation stalled while the bowls and platters were cleared away and a pear and cardamon torte was served.

"I'm not going to ask you to not tell anyone or to not publish it," Meredith said. "I trust that after you know the whole story, you will see why we wish to keep Colin's work during the war a secret, and you will do what is best."

"Okay." Charley helped herself to another cup of coffee.

"You are right about our father being a member of the *Ossewabrandwag*. He refused to allow Christo—sorry, when I think of that time, I forget and use my brother's true name. I need to be more careful. Our father refused to allow *Colin* to enlist."

"Your brother wanted to join the Allies?"

Meredith nodded. "Very much. It was a point of honour for him. But our father was cold and domineering, more so after Mother died."

"Instead, he sent your brother to Europe with diamonds to help the Fuhrer."

"And he sent me away to boarding school in neutral Switzerland, yes." She poked at her torte but didn't eat any of it. "My father was very clever, always scheming. He didn't realize that Colin was equally clever, maybe more so, given how everything turned out."

Charley put her fork down and leaned in closer. "How so?"

"My father's contacts in Germany were tenuous—someone who said they knew someone, who knew someone...you understand? He supported the regime but the *Ossewabrandwag*'s activities were pretty much limited to South Africa. When Colin was sent to Europe, our father expected him to sort out how best to use the diamonds to help the Nazis. But once there, my brother sought out the French resistance fighters and made his way to those in command in Europe. The diamonds were used to help the Allies. After the war, in appreciation for his assistance, he was given the opportunity to settle in the country of his choice. He'd met some Canadians and planned to move to Alberta. He liked the idea of living among the mountains. But when he came to get me, I had seen pictures of Kingston and the lake, and I asked if we could move here, instead."

"Why did you change your names if he was a hero? Why hide who you were?" Charley asked. "It couldn't be because you were afraid of your father. He'd killed himself." She winced at how hard-hearted it sounded, but Meredith didn't look upset, so she continued. "And the *Ossewabrandwag* doesn't exist anymore."

"Changing our names is partly my brother's desire to erase the awful part of our past, but also because he is still fearful some part of it will come back to hurt us. He was quite distraught to realize you'd figured out who he was. He'd thought he'd covered his tracks very effectively."

"He seemed to take it all very calmly," Charley said, remembering his initial reaction. "But you can tell him, your identities were discovered through a school photograph of you. Dan had mentioned you'd gone to school in Switzerland and Grace, our researcher, tracked you down there. She compared the engagement photograph we published with various private schools' yearbooks. If you want to talk about dogged..."

Meredith dabbed her eyes with her napkin. "He'll be relieved." She raised her head and unsuccessfully tried to force a smile. "But for me, it means I have to remove another part of my past. I will no longer be able to mention Switzerland and my time there."

"I'm so sorry." Charley's heart ached for the young woman who had already given up so much. She glanced around the room. Or had she? She was living in a mansion and was engaged to be married to a well-respected member of Kingston society. That was surprisingly good for a twenty-year-old immigrant, considering the plight of so many who'd been displaced by the war.

"So, you see now why we've kept our past a secret."

"Not entirely," Charley said. "If your brother gave the diamonds to the Allies, where did you get the money to buy this house? To purchase half of downtown Kingston?"

Meredith frowned. "Yes. This is the part he is least proud of. He did give all his diamonds to the Allies, but I was sent to Switzerland with diamonds of my own—well, not mine specifically, but they were sewn into my clothes for safe-keeping. Our father thought of it as insurance in case he lost the mine to his political foes. Which he did."

"And you didn't declare them when you came to Canada," Charley guessed.

"No. Colin was afraid the Allies would think he'd been holding back on them during the war, and we'd be sent back to South Africa." She stared earnestly at Charley. "He didn't even know I had them until he came to get me and bring me to Canada."

"And his involvement with the Tassisti Social Club and the west-end development?"

"They are as he said. He thought he was helping a tenant by writing to the minister to support the club. He had no idea it was involved in anything illegal. And he's withdrawn from the development proposal for the same reason."

Charley was slowly digesting the information. She wasn't entirely convinced Meredith was being truthful about her brother's virtue. Would a savvy businessman allow his name to appear on a charter without checking its legitimacy? And it was as likely he'd withdrawn from the development proposal because she and Lester were getting too close to exposing its connection to a gambling syndicate.

And what about Dan? What better way of ensuring your safety than by backing an up-and-coming politician and marrying him off to your sister?

"I can see I've failed to convince you." Meredith frowned.

"I'm not unconvinced, either. Being overly suspicious is a hazard of my job. I will keep your secret for now, but I can't promise that I won't expose you if I find you've lied to me." Charley pushed back her chair and stood. "Thank you for brunch."

"I am glad you came," Meredith said, rising with her. "I'll have the car brought around for you."

In the foyer, Charley thanked the housekeeper for her assistance with her coat. She accepted her hat and turned to say goodbye to her hostess.

"I have one more request," Meredith said. "Dan and I have set our wedding date. It is going to be here, on Christmas Eve."

Charley's breath caught in her throat. *So soon?*

"We'd like you to be there."

"THIS COFFEE IS SO GOOD." Laine took another sip from her mug.

"Speaking of good coffee, I had brunch with Meredith Banks yesterday," Charley said. "She invited me to their wedding. It's going to be Christmas Eve."

"That soon?"

Charley nodded and took another sip from her mug.

"Are you okay with it?" Laine asked. Her speech was improving but each word continued to be a challenge. By the end of the day, she'd be exhausted, reduced to one-word responses.

"Yeah, I'm fine."

"And yet, you look troubled."

Charley heaved a sigh and set her mug down on the bedside table. "It's this story I'm working on for the *Trib*. There are so many threads to it, and it leads to so many suspects."

"Would it help to talk it out?"

"Oh, Laine, thanks, but I don't want to burden you."

"Not a burden. I like helping you. Makes me feel useful."

Charley smiled at her friend. In the past, Laine's medical insight had proved invaluable to her. Freddie said her mind was still sharp; it was the verbal expression of her thoughts that she found difficult.

Charley had spent most of the weekend going over and over what she knew, what she thought she knew, and what was still missing. She'd hoped talking with Mark and Lester would have helped, but it had just added another layer to the mystery—Adams was Lester's source in the police department, and yet...

She felt she was going round and round in circles. Perhaps, having to explain it out loud would help. "Okay. Here's what I know."

Charley started at the beginning with the death of anti-development Alderman Smythe and the election of pro-development Alderman Carruthers, and how it affected the developers' lobbying to increase the size of the city's annexation proposal coming before the city council. Then there was the raid on the Tassisti Social Club, the death of Raymond Palmer, the abduction of baby Anthony, and the involvement of Colin Banks in both plans to develop the west-end and with Tassisti. And finally, there was Dan's disclosure that Constable Adams was a partner in the purchase of the hotel Lester had mentioned in his first article.

"I think Adams is nothing more than a lackey who's being paid off," Charley said. "It's who's calling the shots that I want to know."

"Grace says Banks is a bad man," Laine said. "Traitor. Diamonds."

It didn't surprise Charley that Grace would talk to Laine about her work, but Grace didn't know the whole story—at least Meredith's version of it. Tempted as she was to ask Grace to verify it, she'd keep her promise and remain silent for now. It did occur to her, however, that Colin wasn't the only clever one in the Banks family. Meredith had proven to be very cunning herself. And given that, Charley couldn't completely rule out the possibility that she was involved, too.

Great. Another suspect.

"Banks is hiding a shady background, that's true. But is he the mastermind behind this?" Charley asked. "He swears he was duped into having his name on the Tassisti charter, and his sister says he's withdrawn his investment in the west-end development."

"Others?" Laine prompted.

"Arcadi and Bigelow."

"Your driver?"

"Yeah." Charley topped up Laine's mug from the thermos she'd brought and poured the rest into hers. "He's the one who worries me most." She hadn't thought much about it at first, but after listening to Lester talk about the challenges of making a living with a family she started to wonder how it was that Romeo Arcadi could raise four children, pay off his mortgage, and buy out the other taxi drivers in the co-operative—all at a time when the country was mired in an economic depression. He said he'd written to the province to cancel Tassisti's charter, but Grace hadn't been able to confirm it. Mark said he'd try to find out more from a contact he had at the provincial police's anti-gambling branch, but so far, he'd come up empty, too.

"Seems nice, though," Laine said.

"Too nice, maybe. He's managed to fool Gran, which surprises me. She's usually a better judge of character."

"Bigelow?"

"No, I don't think so. If you'd seen him, you'd under-stand. The poor wretch is paralyzed from the neck down. A car accident a few years ago. He can't move and can barely even speak."

"Not the neck." Laine's eyes narrowed.

"Not the neck what?"

"Can he move his head?" Laine leaned forward.

Charley thought back to their meeting. "Yeah, I'm sure of it."

Laine frowned. "Describe in detail, please."

"He's tall but has obviously been confined to a wheelchair for some years because I could see how skinny his legs had become underneath his trousers. He was still broad-shouldered—"

"Arms? Did you see them? Skinny too?" Laine interrupted.

"No, I didn't see them. He was wrapped up in a blanket."

"Hunched over?"

"No, he was sitting up straight."

"Strapped in?"

"I don't think so. At least..." Charley took a moment to think about what she'd seen. "No, I am quite certain he was sitting up on his own."

"Breathing?"

Charley chuckled. "Of course he was breathing."

Laine huffed in annoyance. "On his own?"

"Oh, yes, he was breathing on his own. He was coughing a lot, though. Sounded like a smoker's cough, but I don't see how that's possible unless he has someone holding his cigs for him." Charley imagined it would be possible, but his housemother hadn't seemed the sort. However, Bigelow would need someone to feed him, so maybe her initial impression of the woman had been uncharitable. "Why all the questions?"

"Not paralyzed at the neck." Laine shook her head. "Very unlikely."

"Why?"

"Wouldn't be able to sit up on his own. No control. Probably not breathe on his own, either."

"Do you think he was faking it?"

"When was the accident?"

"I don't know exactly, but it was 1945. Grace found a reference to it in the Hamilton newspaper."

Laine nodded. "Give me a date and hospital. I will call to confirm injuries."

"Can you do that?" Charley asked.

Laine's blue eyes twinkled. "Grace is a good teacher."

Is Bigelow faking?

Charley was mulling over the implications as she left the hospital and turned west to walk to the *Tribune*.

"Mrs. Hall!"

She glanced across the street to see Romeo Arcadi standing beside his cab, waving at her. "I'll walk," she called back and hastened her pace away from him.

What is he doing here?

It was unnerving when she considered the number of times he'd appeared out of nowhere to offer her a ride. How did he always seem to know where to find her? Why hadn't she thought it was suspicious before?

If Bigelow was feigning the severity of his paralysis, Arcadi had to know about it. They'd been friends—partners —for years. How could Bigelow keep up such an elaborate pretense without accomplices?

A hand grabbed her arm in a vice-like grip, forcing her to stop. "Ow!" She whirled around, her heart pounding.

"You must come with me." Arcadi's dark eyes stared intensely out from under his cap.

"I said 'I'll walk'." She wrenched her arm, but the wiry cabbie's grip held firm.

He hustled her across the street, flung open the driver's door of his taxi, and pushed her inside.

THIS CAN'T BE HAPPENING.

Before she had a chance to react, Arcadi had slid in beside her, started the engine, and was hurtling into traffic.

She pressed open the cab's door determined to leap to safety, but they were moving too quickly. She risked a glance back at Arcadi, which was a mistake. The delay cost her. He leaned over and pulled the door closed.

"Don't do that," he said, pressing down on the accelerator. "Are you trying to kill yourself?"

"Slow down, then." She tried to sound confident, but her hands were trembling. "Where are you taking me anyway?"

"Somewhere we can talk."

"Why couldn't we talk on the street?"

Arcadi glanced at her and then eased his foot off the gas pedal. "Why are you so afraid?" He sounded confused.

"Oh, I don't know," she said, trying to gauge whether or not he'd slowed down enough for her to jump out of the cab without risking serious injury. *Not yet.* "Maybe it's because you forced me into your taxi and are driving like a maniac."

He turned onto a gravel road near the old fort and stopped at the waterfront.

Charley gripped the door handle, ready to run. But

where? They were a good quarter mile from the main road. She couldn't see anyone around.

"I would never hurt you, Mrs. Hall."

"My bruised arm tells a different story."

He swore in Italian and slammed his fist into the dashboard.

Charley had been a reporter long enough to have picked up a few words in the various dialects of the immigrant populations. Curse words were at the top of the list.

Arcadi gripped the steering wheel and lowered his forehead to it.

Now would be a good time to make a break for it.

She didn't move. Something was going on here and she was curious to know what it was.

"I'll be fine," she said, surprised to find herself offering her kidnapper reassurance.

He turned toward her. "I did not mean to scare you. Sometimes I react without thinking." He shrugged.

"Like when you slugged that Mountie with a baseball bat?" Charley asked.

"I am not a violent man. You were in danger. That is all."

"Am I in danger now?"

"Not from me."

She angled herself so they were face-to-face and was struck by how weary he looked. Arcadi was in his fifties, but he'd always seemed younger, more energetic and effervescent than other men his age. Now there were dark circles under his eyes and creases at the corners of his mouth. "Maybe you'd better tell me what's going on."

"After I took you and Detective Spadina to visit Paulie I started asking some of the drivers from the old co-op days questions about him—well, about Tassisti, actually. I originally set it up because I knew it was important for the drivers to have a place to go and relax—to be with other drivers. This was what we did in the Old Country."

It was the first time he'd ever spoken about where he'd come from. Since he had no accent, Charley had always assumed he'd been born in Canada. It wasn't until she had Grace look him up that she'd discovered he'd immigrated after the Great War.

"Italy," she said.

He nodded. "I didn't drive a taxi there, of course, but it is the same with any business."

"Why did you come to Canada?" she asked.

He cocked his head to the side as though taken aback by her question. "It is of no consequence," he said, finally. "What is important is Tassisti. I was married and had a family so even though I helped start it, I rarely went there. Paulie was the one who took care of things."

"He was treasurer of the co-op and the club?"

"Yes. What I've recently learned is that some of the card games weren't always friendly penny games. Paulie encouraged some of the younger men to wager much larger sums. A lot of the drivers were afraid of him."

"And you didn't know any of this?"

Arcadi glanced down. "I should have."

"Do you think he deliberately didn't file the final tax return to cancel the club's charter?"

"I don't know. Forgetting something like that is not like him. He was always meticulous—especially with money. But it would have been around the time of his accident, so he may be telling the truth."

"What can you tell me about his accident?"

"Not much more than what he's already told you. The year was 1945 and he was returning from a Thanksgiving

Day visit to his family in Hamilton when his car was struck by a truck. He spent months in hospital."

"Did you visit him? Do you remember which hospital it was?"

"It was in Toronto, that's all I remember. I went once, right after I heard about it. He was in pretty bad shape."

"Fully paralyzed?"

"That's what Louisa said."

"Louisa?"

"You met her briefly. She owns the boarding house. They aren't married—her and Paulie—but they've been together for years."

"Do you think he's capable of running a gambling syndicate?" Charley asked.

"Do you? Look at him. He can't move, can barely speak. That cough of his, I am sure is because he can't get enough air in his lungs."

He shouldn't be able to get any air in his lungs, according to Laine, but Charley kept that thought to herself. "But you're suspicious anyway?"

"Troubled. I am unsettled by the stories I heard from some of the drivers. And I am worried for your safety if you continue to pursue this story."

"I appreciate your concern. I'll be careful," she said.

"It would be better if you dropped it altogether."

TROUBLED WAS ALSO how Charley felt after Arcadi dropped her off at the *Trib*.

What was the point of that conversation? Was Arcadi trying to cover up his own involvement by throwing suspicion on Bigelow? Was he trying to scare her off the story?

First Meredith and now Arcadi? Did everyone think she was a patsy who could be manipulated?

Or were they telling the truth?

She was surprised to see Lester in the newsroom. He looked up from his typewriter as she approached his desk. "Oh good, Hall, you're here."

"I'm surprised you are. Who is staying with Eleanor?"

"Emerson is there this morning. I came by to clear up a few things and talk to Mr. Sherman. Miss Fletcher says she has some information for us, but she won't reveal it until we are both present."

Charley smiled to herself as she followed Lester back to the morgue. She loved Grace.

"Hello, you two," Grace greeted them each with a cup of tea. "Have a seat and hold onto your hats."

"Is it that good?" Charley asked.

"I've done some digging into Adams. And the first thing you're going to want to know is that the letter from the bank is a fake."

"How do you know that?" Charley asked.

"I called the bank pretending to be the secretary for the hotel owner's lawyer. I said our client had lost the letter regarding Constable Adams' financing and asked for a copy. Adams isn't a client of that bank."

"Maybe you got the bank wrong," Lester said to Charley.

"No, I recognized the letterhead immediately. There are only so many banks in Kingston. I am quite sure I didn't make a mistake."

"It doesn't matter anyway," Grace said. "To be thorough, I called the others with the same story and got the same result."

"How is that possible? Adams must bank somewhere?" Charley said. "Did you try the credit unions?"

"Yes. I've spent most of the morning on the telephone. As far as I can tell, Adams doesn't have a Kingston bank account."

"Do you know where he's from?" Lester asked.

"Madoc," Grace said, referring to a village about sixty miles northwest of Kingston.

"Maybe he has an account at a bank there," Lester said.

"It doesn't matter, though, does it?" Charley looked at him in exasperation. "The point is the letter from the bank is a forgery."

Lester scratched his head. "Yeah, I guess that's right," he said but without conviction.

"I wonder if Palmer knew and that was why it was in the file?" Charley took a sip of her tea. "I'm still not sure why you put anything about the hotel in your article in the first place. Did Palmer mention it to you?" she asked Lester.

"As a clarification. We originally thought it was part of the west-end development, remember? He said it was going to be a purchase of an existing hotel." A furrow formed between his brows and he frowned. "Come to think of it, I am sure he mentioned it would become a matter for city council to deal with, which is why it was included. I could go check my notes, but, yes, I'm quite certain that was what he said."

"But Dan...Alderman Cannon told me a private sale like that would never come before the council," Charley said.

"Perhaps Palmer suspected the sale was related to the gambling syndicate," Charley said. "If the city is planning to crack down on these types of establishments, a hotel purchased with gambling proceeds would be part of it."

"The west-end proposal comes before council on Wednesday. I'm going to go over it with a fine-tooth comb. And I'm going to review all my notes again." Lester took a final swallow of his tea and handed Grace his cup.

"You should also check for an updated list of investors. I've heard a rumour that Colin Banks has withdrawn," Charley said.

Lester's eyes widened in surprise. "That's a story worth pursuing."

"My thought exactly," Charley agreed. Given Lester's feelings about Banks, he'd be more than thorough. And if he happened to find anything to disprove Meredith's story, well, that would be fine with Charley.

"I better get on it. Emerson has a job this afternoon and I don't want to leave Ellie by herself. All she does—all we both do, when I'm home—is sit by the phone hoping and praying we'll hear s-s-something...a-a-about...Anthony..." He shuddered, took a deep breath and stood shakily. "Ladies."

Charley watched Lester return to the newsroom. She was amazed at how well he seemed to be holding up, but how much more could he take? Baby Anthony had been missing for six days.

She turned back to Grace. "I saw Laine this morning and we discussed the case. She has a hunch, but we need you to do some digging for us." Charley waited for Grace to pour her another cup of tea. "We need you to find what you can about an accident that occurred in or around Toronto, Thanksgiving 1945. Paul Bigelow's car was hit by a truck and he was seriously injured. If you can find out what hospital he went to, Laine thinks she can get hold of his medical records."

"Bigelow? This is the guy who's paralyzed?"

"Partially paralyzed, Laine thinks."

"Okay then." Grace jotted down a few notes and then looked up at Charley. "I've got something else you're going to find interesting."

"It's like Christmas already with you handing out all sorts of goodies."

"This one's a doozie. You better sit down."

Charley propped herself up on one of the stools beside the large worktable. "Okay, hit me."

"I found out something very interesting about Romeo Arcadi. When he bought his house in 1921, he had a co-signer for the mortgage."

"Paul Bigelow?" Charley guessed.

"Frederick Stormont II."

"And you brought me here why?" Mark extended his hand to help Charley out of his car.

"To help me talk to Gran."

"You want *me* to help you talk to *your* grandmother. Are you five years old?"

"Very funny." She batted away his hand and exited the vehicle unaided. "You know what she's like. She doesn't tell me anything. She likes you. I'm hoping if you're here, she'll be less inclined to put us off."

Charley had asked Mark to pick her up at the *Tribune*. She'd used the short ride from the newspaper to her home to brief him on her conversations with Laine, Arcadi, and Grace.

"You've been a busy beaver, haven't you?" he'd teased, but he sounded impressed.

"Is my grandmother here?" Charley asked as Rachel took their coats.

"Which one? Lady Thorton has gone out for her daily constitutional and Mrs. Stormont is in the drawing room."

She scowled as Mark chuckled at Rachel's subtle dig.

"Detective!" Bessie looked up from her book as they entered the drawing room. "How lovely to see you again.

Do I take it from your presence here that you have somehow managed to get back into my granddaughter's good graces?"

"It's lovely to see you, too, Bessie," Mark said plopping himself on the sofa beside her. "I am not sure I have been forgiven my transgression, but she needs my assistance and so here I am."

Mark's ease with Gran irked her. She had every right to be furious with Mark. He'd accused her of using the possibility of Theo's return as an excuse to not marry Dan all the while knowing her husband couldn't possibly still be alive. It was cruel, but Dan had made the same argument to her over and over again—although perhaps not quite as bluntly. Since their falling out, her temper had mellowed until the allegation had become nothing more than another of Mark's opinions that irritated more than incensed.

It was his statement to Gran about coming to her aid that stung. It reminded her of Dan's complaint about how she used him—took advantage of their friendship—for her own benefit, implying that she gave nothing in return. She didn't think that was true. After all, she'd been the one who'd found the evidence to prove Dan's innocence when he was charged with murder.

Once again, Mark and Dan had made the same point, so why did the detective's words slice through to her core and lay bare insecurities she never knew she had?

"Charlotte!"

Charley jumped. "Sorry, I didn't hear what you said."

"I said 'sit down'." Bessie frowned. "You looked like you were lost in the clouds. Is something wrong?"

"No, Gran, nothing." She pushed away her concerns about Mark and his recriminations and did as her grandmother told her.

"Now, I don't imagine this is purely a social call," Bessie

said, shifting her gaze between Charley and Mark. "Who is going to tell me why you're here?"

"Romeo Arcadi," Charley said.

"Not this again. Charlotte, I told you, you are being ridiculous to suspect him of some nefarious deed."

"It's not 'some nefarious deed'. It's possibly murder and kidnapping, but that's not what we're here to ask about." Charley ignored her grandmother's muttered "preposterous" and proceeded. "What is—was—his relationship with my father?"

Bessie exhaled. "I see."

"So, you know about it?"

"A little. Mr. Arcadi is an immensely proud man and he wouldn't thank me for sharing his personal business, but I don't think you're going to let this go until I tell you what I know, are you?" She looked down her nose with disapproval. "All right, then. After the war, the Great War, your parents were involved with helping new immigrants settle in our community. Mr. Arcadi was one of them."

"By helping them, you mean giving them money?"

"In some cases money. Sometimes jobs. They offered whatever aid they could."

"My father co-signed Mr. Arcadi's mortgage."

"As well as many others'." Bessie nodded. "And in his will, he left a sizable sum of money to be shared among many of the families he'd helped, including Mr. Arcadi's."

"Sizable? Enough to pay off a mortgage?"

Gran nodded.

"For many families?"

"It was important to him. And we supported that decision."

Her father had died in 1923. He couldn't possibly have known that in less than a decade the country would be plunged into an economic depression and that her grandfather would end up selling his beloved *Tribune*. Would he have been able to keep the newspaper if her father hadn't given away so much of the family's money? Would Grandpa still be alive?

Charley chided herself for her moment of selfishness. She had no reason to feel sorry for herself. What her parents had done in sharing their wealth was admirable—something to be proud of.

"Wait!" She sat up sharply. "I've read everything that was written after their deaths—all their charitable causes—and there was no mention of them giving money to others like that."

"Of course not. Your parents would never allow any publicity around what they had done. These were proud families. They weren't looking to take advantage. They simply needed a little help to get started. It was all done very privately to maintain their dignity."

"Getting back to Romeo Arcadi and his self-appointed role as Charley's personal chauffeur..." Mark interjected.

"What about it?" Bessie said.

"Did you ask him to do that?" Charley said.

"No. I had no idea his was one of the families your parents helped until he introduced himself after he drove us home from the Dominion Day tea a few months ago. He told me he was filling in for one of his drivers when he took your first call. He realized who you were and was uncomfortable with where you insisted on being dropped off. After that, he took it upon himself to look out for you. That's all."

"How does he always manage to appear where I am? Is he spying on me?"

"That's not hard to figure out," Mark said. "He has drivers all over the city."

"So, he *is* spying on me."

"I am sure if you asked him to stop, he would," Bessie said. "But frankly, I feel reassured knowing there is someone we can trust keeping an eye on you."

"It's creepy."

"Nevertheless, it does explain a lot about the man and how he was able to buy the taxi co-op," Mark said.

"Do you still think he's a suspect?" Charley asked.

"Everyone's a suspect until they're not," Mark said. He turned to Bessie. "Have you ever heard of Arcadi's friend Paul Bigelow?"

"That's not a name I've heard before." She cocked her ear at a commotion in the hallway. "I do believe Evelyn has returned."

Charley leapt to her feet. "In that case, we should get going."

"But I haven't had the pleasure of meeting your other grandmother."

Charley glared at Mark and then whirled around as Evelyn marched briskly into the room.

Too late now.

"Hello." Evelyn's face was flushed from the cold and strands of her white hair branched out of her head like an unruly bush.

"You must be Lady Thorton," Mark said. He stood and offered his hand.

Gran made the introductions and Evelyn sat down. Resigned, Charley followed suit.

"A real detective? How exciting," Evelyn said. "You do have that Sam Spade look about you."

"I've not seen the films, but I have been told I resemble Humphrey Bogart." He gave her his dazzling smile. "Although considerably taller."

Charley snorted earning a glower of reprimand from Gran. But really? Humphrey Bogart?

Then again, there was something ominous about Mark that lurked just under the surface. She hadn't forgotten how threatened he'd made her feel when they first met—still could when he was in a dark mood. He had the demeanour of an ordinary man and yet everything about him was extraordinary. Not terribly unlike the Sam Spade character Bogart played in *The Maltese Falcon*.

Rachel carried in a tray with a teapot and several cups and placed it on the sideboard. Before she began pouring, she handed Charley a slip of paper. "Miss Fletcher telephoned and asked me to deliver this message to you."

Charley unfolded the note.

"Laine says paralysis is from hips down."

IT WOULD BE an understatement to say that Constable Marillo was skeptical when Charley and Mark offered their theory about the City Hall deaths. He'd been adamant that Adams couldn't possibly be involved. The only reason he'd even agreed to go with them to visit Paul Bigelow was to search the boarding house for baby Anthony—and only after he'd berated them for not contacting the police when the baby was first abducted.

But as they watched Adams, dressed in his civvies, descend the steps of the boarding house and get into his vehicle to drive away, Charley had no temptation to claim, "I told you so." From the back seat of the police cruiser she could see Marillo's eyes in the rear-view mirror as they first registered surprise, then disappointment and, finally, resignation.

"So much for calling in sick," she heard Mark mutter, but even he couldn't keep the note of disappointment out of his voice. A dirty cop was something no one had wanted to believe.

"All right, let's go." Marillo reached for the door handle, but Mark stopped him.

"Wait a minute." Mark pointed toward another vehicle that had pulled up in front of the house.

For the second time in as many moments, Charley felt a wave of disappointment as she watched Romeo Arcadi get out of his cab and climb the steps to the boarding house's front porch. She had so wanted Gran to be right.

"Okay, now we'll go," Mark said as Arcadi disappeared into the house.

Charley took a closer look at the woman who answered the door. She hadn't paid much attention to Louisa during their first visit. She looked to be in her mid-to-late fifties with choppy grey hair and a dour, unforgiving face. She'd been baking, judging from the handprints of flour on her apron.

"Whaddaya want?" She scowled at Marillo, who had taken the lead.

"We're here to see Paul Bigelow. I presume he's in."

"'Course he is." She huffed and led them into the sitting room.

Romeo Arcadi jumped to his feet at their arrival. "Mrs. Hall, what are you doing here?" He sounded distressed.

She ignored him and focused her attention on the man in the wheelchair.

Paul Bigelow's back was to them, but he rotated his head and shifted his shoulders and upper body, which he shouldn't have been able to do. She took a step closer and thought she detected some movement underneath the blanket that was wrapped around his upper torso and covered his lap.

Laine's suspicions confirmed, she turned back to Arcadi. "How long have you known?"

"Charley." Mark's warning was a low whisper.

She glanced over and saw that the card players from their previous visit had left their game and were slowly moving into the room. Louisa remained by the entrance, blocking access back to the hallway. Mark and Marillo had strategically positioned themselves against a wall across from each other, protecting their backs. Charley, standing in the centre of the room, was vulnerable. She took a cautious step backward.

"I didn't know until today," Arcadi said. "I—"

Bigelow's wheelchair whirled around. He's pushed the blanket away and was pointing a gun at her. "You are too nosy by far," he said, cocking the gun.

"No, Paulie!" Arcadi leapt forward and pushed Charley to the ground as the bullet ripped through the room.

She bucked against the weight of Arcadi, but the cabbie held her in place. "Keep still!" he hissed.

In the centre of the room the three thugs had formed a phalanx around Bigelow, their handguns drawn. Charley craned her neck to see that both Marillo and Mark were pointing their revolvers toward the group. No one was moving.

"I believe we've reached a stalemate," Marillo said.

"I think you're mistaken, officer." Bigelow's formerly reedy voice had disappeared, and he spoke with clear authority. "Look around. You're outmanned."

"I don't know," Mark said. "I'm a rather good shot. I bet I could pop two of your guys before they got off one."

"Such bravado, Detective. But then that's what I would expect from you Toronto types."

Bigelow nodded toward his men and Charley heard a pistol cocking.

"What have you got against Toronto?" Mark asked.

"Who do you think did this to me?" Bigelow replied.

"Ah, competitors. Let me guess, they didn't like the idea of you setting up shop here in Kingston."

"They got theirs. Payback for this and more."

"Who are your backers?" Mark asked. "I know you're working for a bigger group. Montreal? Oh wait. Hamilton, right? I heard there was a nasty crew operating out of Steeltown."

"Enough! Let's end this."

Charley heard a thump and everyone turned toward the entrance of the room. Louisa had disappeared.

Pop! Pop!

Two of the thugs fell to the ground.

A flurry of shots followed. She could see a pair of dark green trousers pause in front of her. She squirmed against Arcadi—neither Mark nor Marillo were wearing green—and then she heard "Keep her safe." She knew that voice.

Adams.

"Watch out!" That was Mark.

Another shot reverberated around the room and Adams fell to the ground. She could see his face, not two feet away, staring back at her, looking royally peeved.

Two more shots.

Then silence.

Arcadi rolled off of her and she struggled to her knees.

Across the room, Mark was placing a pair of handcuffs on one of the thugs who lay prone on the floor. The other two must be dead.

Bigelow was slumped in his chair, immobile. She held her breath as Mark approached him and wrenched the gun out of his hand. Bigelow offered no resistance. Dead, too, then. Mark dug around the body and found a second revolver hidden under the wheelchair's seat and tucked it into his belt.

Where's Marillo?

She heard a disturbance in the hallway and then the

constable pushed Louisa into the room, her hands secured behind her back. The bedraggled woman stumbled to Bigelow's wheelchair. Then, oddly, she turned her back to it and squatted, awkwardly trying to dig around the body with her cuffed hands.

"It's not there," Mark said, pointing to the revolver in his belt.

Louisa let loose a string of expletives as she collapsed on the ground.

"How you doing, buddy?" Marillo said from behind her. *Adams!*

She whirled around to see the constable kneeling beside his partner.

"I...g-guess...I...blew...m-m-my...cover." Adams' voice was breathy, and Charley could barely make out the words.

"No one move!"

Three uniformed officers rushed into the room, guns pointed.

"You're a little late," Mark said.

They lowered their weapons. Sergeant Kearn glanced toward Marillo but went to speak with Mark.

"Adams! Adams!" There was panic in Marillo's voice. "Ron. Stay with me, buddy. Hang in there. Ronnie!"

Charley tried to stand—she wanted to go to Adams, help Marillo if she could. But the room tumbled before her eyes and she sank back down to the floor.

Kearn and the two officers hurried to Adams' side. But they were all too late.

Marillo rose and lunged toward the prone thug—the one left alive—and began brutally kicking him. None of the officers moved to stop him. It was Mark who pulled him back. "You don't want to do that."

Marillo glared at him, gave the man one more punt, and stalked away.

Charley tried to rise again. Her legs were so shaky she prayed they would hold. Arcadi offered his arm in support and she took it gratefully, ignoring his "tsks" as she led him over to Louisa. "Where is the baby?" she demanded.

Louisa looked up, her eyes dark with hate, and spit at Charley.

"What baby?" Kearn asked.

"I haven't got to that part yet," Mark told him.

"Davidson. Connolly. Search the house," Kearn ordered.

"I'll go with you," Charley said.

"Absolutely not!" Kearn declared. "We don't know if someone's still hiding here."

"How did you know to come here?" Charley asked.

"Adams called the station and spoke directly with the captain," Kearn said. "Seems he spotted you three and was afraid you were about to get yourselves into trouble. Captain was the only one who knew what he'd been up to. Adams was supposed to wait for us to arrive before going in."

"If he'd waited, we'd be dead," Mark said bluntly.

"Typical Adams," Marillo said in a ragged voice. "Always angling to be the hero."

Charley lifted the crocheted purple afghan off the back of the chair and covered Adams' body with it. It seemed the least she could do.

Adams hadn't been a dirty cop. And Arcadi hadn't known that Bigelow was faking the severity of his paralysis. She should be relieved. The bad guys had been caught. So why was she still feeling a suffocating sense of doom?

By the time Davidson and Connolly returned from

searching the boarding house, more uniformed and plain-clothed officers had arrived, and Louisa and the thug had been taken away. The two cops didn't need to say anything. Charley knew the horrible truth from their tightly drawn faces.

Baby Anthony isn't here.

CHARLEY WAS EXHAUSTED, bone weary in mind and body. She'd spent the last two hours giving her statement on everything she knew and suspected about Paul Bigelow along with his involvement in what the police now admitted were the murders of Alderman Smythe and Raymond Palmer.

Based on evidence Constable Adams had amassed, the anti-gambling branch of the provincial police had rounded up other men suspected of being members of Bigelow's crew. Alderman Carruthers was on the list. Colin Banks was not. With Louisa and the thug keeping mum, she hoped the police would find a weak link among the new suspects and someone would tell them where to find baby Anthony.

"Is Mark—I mean, Detective Spadina still being interviewed?" She hadn't seen him since she'd left the boarding house with Sergeant Kearn.

"Well, that's a very interesting question," Sergeant Kearn said, helping her slip into her coat. "*Mister* Spadina has not made himself available to us as of yet. If you know where he is, I'd suggest you inform him that we are quite anxious to speak with him, and it's not a request."

Charley spotted Arcadi waiting for her as she stepped out of the interview room. She held onto his arm as he escorted her out of the police station. She was too tired to worry about Mark now. The man would do as he pleased when he pleased.

Arcadi held open the back door of his cab for her, but Charley opened the front door and took the seat beside his. If he was surprised, the cabbie didn't show it. He rounded the taxi and slid in beside her.

"I owe you an apology," she said. "I thought you were tied up with Bigelow in this mess, and I was wrong."

Arcadi put the cab in gear and pulled out onto the darkened, deserted street. "It was understandable."

"I couldn't figure out why you were always available to drive me and why you wouldn't accept a fare. And then when..." She was babbling. She stopped and took a deep breath and started again. "I know you knew my father."

He nodded. "I figured your curiosity and that clever mind of yours would get the better of you eventually."

"Except it didn't. I didn't look into you because I wanted to know why you were driving me around for free; I did it because of this case. Because of the Tassisti Social Club and the gambling."

"You're a good reporter and I was part of the story."

She glanced out the window and realized he'd turned north, into the business section of town. "Where are we going?"

"A friend of yours asked me to take you to meet him."

What friend?

"Anyway," she continued, "I wanted to let you know that any debt you feel you owed to my father is more than repaid. You don't have to always be at my beck-and-call. If I need to hire a car, I can do it like everyone else."

Arcadi glanced over at her and tsked. "I am afraid that will not be possible. A father's obligation can never be discharged. And since your father cannot be here to look out for you, I consider it my duty and my honour to do so on his behalf."

"Well, that's ridiculous. You have a family of your own to look after."

"Yes, a very lovely family, thank you very much. Four children. Three of whom are married with families of their own, and my youngest, Nico, who will make a fine husband someday. Perhaps, you would like to meet him?"

Oh boy.

She stared out the window, watching the dark storefronts pass until she heard Arcadi's turn signal ticking, and he drew his cab to a stop in front of a well-illuminated, and familiar, diner. She accepted his hand as he helped her out of the cab. "Don't wait for me. I'll call if I need a ride home."

She opened the door to Joe's and was immediately overcome by the combined comforts of warmth and delicious aromas, which reminded her she hadn't eaten since breakfast. She'd expected to see Mark sitting at his favourite table in the back, but he wasn't the man who stood and waved for her to join him.

Constable Marillo pulled out a chair for her and then sat across from her. "I hope you don't mind me asking Mr. Arcadi to bring you here. I wanted to talk to you, away from the station."

"No, I don't mind at all. But I am surprised that you know about this place."

He chuckled. "Joe's is Spadina's second office. We often meet here for coffee."

"I didn't realize you'd become so close."

"Close would be an overstatement. I did set him up for an interview to join Kingston PD, though. I thought we could use a detective with big city experience and that he'd appreciate getting back into legitimate police work."

"How did that go?"

"About as well as you'd expect. He ticked off both Sergeant Kearn and Captain Cross with his arrogance."

"Oh dear."

"Yeah." Marillo grinned. "Well, it was bad enough that he referred to Kingston as a backwater town—that type of comment we write off as typical Toronto disdain—but when he stated that our detectives were nothing more than a bunch of rank amateurs who didn't know doodly-squat about running an investigation, well the captain hit the roof and Kearn threw him out of the station." Marillo's laughter echoed around the diner.

Charley could well imagine the scene and joined Marillo, laughing harder than she had in a long time—that it was at Mark's expense made it all the more satisfying.

Once they'd sobered and she'd ordered a ham-and-cheese sandwich, she asked Marillo what he wanted to talk to her about. "I'm assuming it has to do with Constable Adams. I can't tell you how much I regret doubting him."

"You weren't alone. All the evidence seemed to suggest it." He reached under his chair and withdrew a file folder. "Captain Cross lent me this. I have to give it back, but he thought I should know the whole story, and I thought you should, too."

"On or off the record?"

"Off, of course." He pulled the file back.

"Can't blame a gal for trying, can you?" She held out her hand and he handed it over.

The folder contained several typewritten pages, all stamped "CONFIDENTIAL."

"It explains how the gambling syndicate tried to recruit him," Marillo said. "Go ahead and read it."

Statement from Constable Ronald P. Adams
May 6, 1948

On the night of May 5, 1948, Constable Adams, who is a member of the Kingston Police Department, attended the home of Margaret McBride for the purpose of returning a book that he had borrowed. The early part of the evening was spent in social intercourse, in the presence of her brother Leo McBride, but after Miss McBride retired, McBride made a veiled suggestion about the possibility of the two of them going into business together. That did not create much impression on Adams.

Later, McBride answered the telephone and he spoke to someone in connection with some sort of a business deal. That, too, did not particularly interest Adams.

When Adams was leaving, McBride suggested he would accompany him, which he did, and suggested they walk along a certain route, which they did. Having separated, Adams continued on his way alone until suddenly a car pulled up to the curb and the headlights were turned off. It was driven by Arthur Carruthers. He engaged Adams in conversation, inquiring discreetly about his work for the Kingston Police Department. Finally, he said to Adams "Look, we need a friend." Adams, sensing the significant trend of this conversation, indicated that the interview was ended. As they were about to separate, Carruthers suggested that Adams forget about the matter.

On arriving at his home, Adams immediately telephoned Captain Cross and reported the occurrence to him and, on May 6, this confidential written report of the occurrence was prepared and will be delivered to Sergeant Anderson, local representative of the Ontario Provincial Police Department's Anti-Gambling Branch.

It was dated and signed by Constable Adams and witnessed by Captain Cross.

Charley looked up at Marillo. "This was before Alderman Smythe's death. Carruthers hadn't been elected alderman yet."

"Keep reading."

She turned to the next page.

Statement from Constable Ronald P. Adams
May 14, 1948

On May 13, the Kingston Police Department, at the request of the Anti-Gambling Branch, raided the Centre Road Club. Carruthers was there. As usual, everything was in order. When the opportunity presented itself, Carruthers suggested to Adams he should join his "ball team" and pointing to some bets that were being made in which several thousand dollars were at stake said, "How would you like to have that kind of money? This would be peanuts as far as we would be concerned. You and I would make a great team with what you know and my help." Later that same night, Carruthers said to Adams, "If you come on my team you would have a hotel of your own within a year, and be driving a Cadillac, and could say 'To hell with the Department'. All you have to do is phone 'your wife' at this number" - pointing to a telephone nearby. "You know everything that's going on with your outfit."

The next day, Adams reported the occurrence to Captain Cross and together they saw Sergeant Anderson and reported to him. Adams asked that he be permitted to pursue the matter with Carruthers and it was agreed that, due to the danger that other members of the police department had been compromised, the operation would remain known to only the three of them.

This time the statement was signed by Adams, Cross and Anderson.

"So 'your wife' was Paul Bigelow?" Charley asked. Adams wasn't married.

Marillo nodded. "Either him or Louisa. According to the captain, Adams believed they were equal partners."

"Adams never said anything about kidnapping a baby?"

"No, that was news to the captain. He says if he'd known that, they'd have shut down the operation right away."

Charley handed the folder back to Marillo so Gillian could serve her sandwich plate. She gratefully accepted a cup of fresh coffee.

"And how did Raymond Palmer get involved?" Charley asked when they were alone again. "He had a copy of a forged letter from a bank stating that Adams was good for a stake in a hotel."

"The anti-gambling branch needed a trusted contact in City Hall, especially after Carruthers was elected. Palmer had been there for years and knew where all the skeletons were hidden."

"And it cost him his life."

Marillo tucked the file back under his chair. "Eat up and then I'll drive you home."

"Can you take me to the *Trib* instead? I need to make sure the Bigelow story gets in the early edition. Sherman will have kittens if we get scooped."

"Here." Grace placed a steaming mug on Charley's desk.

"This isn't tea."

"No, it's coffee—or at least what passes for coffee around here. Do you want me to get you a sandwich? When was the last time you ate?"

Charley took a sip of the coffee. *Blech.* It was stale, probably from the batch she'd brewed in the wee hours of the morning. But at least it was caffeine. "I had a sandwich with Constable Marillo last night."

"Oh, for heaven's sake." Grace glanced around the room and seeing an apple on an empty desk, snagged it and handed it to Charley. "Timmins won't mind."

Charley wasn't so sure, but she took a grateful bite. It was mid-morning and she'd worked all night to get her articles written. The first was a "just-the-facts" version of the round-ups and arrests with a bit of "police-approved" information about the shoot-out she knew the *Whig-Standard* didn't have. Lester would be pleased. The second was a more intimate profile of Constable Ronald P. Adams, full of anecdotes and personal observations of the man. That was the story she was most proud of.

"You should go home and get some sleep," Grace said.

"I'm waiting to hear if the police find out anything about baby Anthony."

"I can call you if anything comes in," Grace said.

"Thank you, but I feel I owe it to Lester to stay here. I can't begin to imagine what he and Eleanor are going through. If holding down the fort for him can help a little, that's what I want to do."

"You're a good friend, Charley."

"Hall!" Sherman hollered from the door to his office.

"Geesh, you'd think he'd be in a better mood after the scoop I gave him," Charley said, pushing back her chair.

"Close the door," Sherman commanded when Charley stepped over the threshold. "Do you want to sit? No? Never mind then." For once, Sherman remained standing, too, although he wouldn't look directly at her. He seemed to take a great interest in his shoes. "Good job on those articles today."

"Thanks."

He cleared his throat. "Uhm, not just today. I have noticed how you've been picking up the slack on the city beat recently."

"I'm always willing go the extra mile for the *Trib*, you know that."

"Well, it's appreciated. And it's been noticed by the publisher, too."

"Nice to know he reads his own newspaper once in a while."

"Oh, he reads it." Sherman walked over to his desk and held up the early edition, covered with red pencil marks. "He makes detailed notes. Every issue."

Charley reached for the newspaper, but Sherman pulled it back. "For my eyes only." He tossed it back onto his desk. "Look, Hall, the reason I asked you in here was to offer you your old job back on the city beat."

Charley took a step backward.

Her old job. This was what she'd wanted for months. This was why she'd agreed to help Lester in the first place.

So why did the thought suddenly make her feel nauseous? Her stomach was somersaulting, and she wished it contained more than an apple and a half-dozen cups of black coffee.

"Hall?"

She held up her hand to stall him. She needed to think. She walked to the sofa and sat down.

What was wrong with her? Why was she even hesitating?

"What about Lester?" she asked. "I thought you said the newspaper couldn't afford both of us on the city beat?"

"Circulation's up and the publisher thinks you two make a good team."

"Who will do the women's pages?" But Charley knew the answer. The former editor, Mildred Preston, had already indicated she'd like to return, having found retirement not to her liking. "Never mind."

"So, it's settled then." Sherman clapped his hands and turned toward his desk, effectively dismissing her.

"No."

Sherman wheeled around. "No?"

"I have a few questions. When you say you and the publisher are happy with my work on the city pages, are you referring to the recent articles I've been writing while Lester's been away? Did you have a problem with what I was writing before he came on staff?"

"I wouldn't say a problem, exactly." Sherman hesitated.

"But your recent work is much more in keeping with the direction the publisher wants the paper to go."

"The new journalism."

"I don't know how 'new' it is, but if that's how you want to refer to it, okay, yes, the new journalism."

"Just the facts. No colour. No opinion."

Sherman pushed his glasses up onto his forehead and he rubbed his eyes. "What are you getting at?"

"Did you like the piece I wrote on Adams?"

Sherman lowered his spectacles. "Sure. It was a great profile. The kid was a real hero."

"But that's not the type of reporting you want for the city beat."

"What do you want, Hall? We ran it on page one, didn't we?"

But that wasn't her issue. Even after she'd been moved to the women's pages, she'd had stories appear on page one —sometimes even above the fold. No, it wasn't a matter of placement, it was much more significant than that.

She didn't want to have to contort her writing style to fit some new idea of what constituted proper journalism in this "changing world." She liked telling people's stories. She liked peppering them with interesting tidbits. The cut-and-dried reporting of just-the-facts didn't appeal to her.

She didn't agree with Lester's assertion that real journalism was objective, the reporter's perspective concealed. The simple act of determining which story was worthy of reporting showed a reporter's bias. It was subtler, certainly, but didn't that make her style of journalism more honest? If Sherman felt her brand of reporting didn't belong on the city beat, then neither did she.

What was it Gran had said? *Wear trousers if you must, but don't succumb to the temptation to behave as men do.*

You truly do your best work and can raise us all—women and men—when you are yourself.

She stood up. "Thank you, Mr. Sherman, but I would prefer to keep my current position as editor of the women's pages."

By the time she got to her desk her whole body was shaking, whether from nervous excitement or extreme hunger she couldn't say. The one thing she did know, however, was that she'd made the right decision.

The telephone sounded and she grabbed it before the second ring.

"Hey, Tiger," Mark's voice rumbled over the line. "Glad you're there."

"Where are you? The police want to speak with you. I can't believe—"

"Hold on. I'm stopped at a service station thirty minutes outside of town. I need you to meet me at Pyne's place, okay?"

"What's going on?"

"Just be there."

CHARLEY TAPPED her foot impatiently on the sidewalk outside of the Pynes' home. What was wrong with her? Mark whistles and she comes running like a faithful puppy? She cringed. And now he was keeping her waiting. Maybe she should go in without him. He hadn't told her not to.

Just when she decided she was too cold to stand around any longer, Mark's dark sedan rounded the corner and pulled to a stop in front of her. It was followed by an unfamiliar police cruiser.

"Hi Tiger," Mark said, coming up beside her. They watched as a uniformed police officer helped a woman holding a baby out of the second vehicle.

"Baby Anthony?" Charley ran toward the woman and peered into the bundle.

"Are you Mrs. Pyne?" The woman pulled the baby closer.

"No, no, she's inside," Charley said excitedly.

"Anthony!" The door to the Pynes' house opened and Eleanor raced down the front steps toward the baby, Lester on her heels.

"That's Mrs. and Mr. Pyne," Charley said.

The woman holding the bundle held it out for examination, and then, satisfied, handed the baby to Eleanor.

Charley's shoulders relaxed as she took in the scene of the family reunited. The shaking had returned, and she could feel a sharp sting on her face as the frosty air hit her tears. She hadn't realized how tense she'd been since the kidnapping. She wiped at them as she watched Eleanor carry the baby into the house, followed by the woman.

After enthusiastically shaking the hands of the officer, Lester rushed over to Mark. "I can't thank you enough, Detective," he said, grabbing Mark's hand. "Where did you find him?"

"Let's go inside." Mark motioned for the officer to join them.

Once settled, Mark introduced Sergeant Homer from Toronto's police department, who had come to make sure the baby they found was indeed Anthony. The woman who'd accompanied them, he said, was a nurse hired to take care of the infant. They'd both be leaving once they were sure the baby was where he belonged.

"Did you get the men who took Anthony?" Lester asked, settling into his chair.

"Where's your wife's brother?" Mark asked him.

"Emerson's at work. I can call the foreman if you need to speak with him."

"I will need to get a statement from him before I leave," Homer said.

Lester turned to Mark, confused. "How is he involved? He's a kid. He's not caught up in any of the shenanigans going on at City Hall."

"I'm afraid Emerson is very much involved," Mark said.

"He didn't take the baby. He's been here with us the whole time. If he knew anything he would have said something. He knows how it's affected his sister." Lester was adamant.

"You're probably right," Homer said. "But I need to speak with him anyway."

"Have you arrested the kidnappers?" Charley asked.

"Kidnapper," Mark said. "Yes, she's in custody."

"She?" Lester and Charley said at the same time.

"Anthony was taken by the woman you know as Linda Fraser," Mark said.

"Linda? No, that's not possible. Not Linda." Lester ran a hand through his sparse hair.

"Are you saying Linda Fraser isn't her real name?" Charley asked.

"No, it's Linda Griffin. She's well known to us," Homer said.

"Linda took Anthony?" Lester didn't seem to be able to comprehend it. "But I thought...then this had nothing to do with the articles we ran in the *Trib*?"

"I was fairly certain from the start that it had nothing to do with Charley's story about Palmer's death or the social club raid. Those guys are killers, not babysitters," Mark said.

"Taking a baby is too much work," Homer agreed.

"What made you suspect Linda?" Charley asked.

"She took off so suddenly—"

"But that was several days before baby Anthony disappeared," Charley said.

"Sure. That's probably why no one thought to mention it at first. It was after I spoke with Emerson later that he told me that he'd been living here with his girlfriend and she'd been pretty upset when he'd ended things with her. I think it took a couple of days for Linda to figure out how to exact her revenge."

"She was so fond of the baby," Lester said. "She was always asking to hold him and help care for him."

"Yes, for what it's worth, she took very good care of

him," Homer said. "When we arrested her, she told us she was very much attached to the baby and she'd taken him to get even with Emerson for ending their relationship."

"I contacted Toronto PD right after I spoke with Emerson and asked them to be on the lookout for her. It took a little longer than I'd hoped for them to find her."

"We'd been searching for her for about six months for breaking parole from Mercer Reformatory. She was released earlier this year after serving nine months for theft," Homer said. "We had no idea she'd been here, in Kingston, all along. Once Spadina let us know she'd likely gone back to Toronto, it was only a matter of time before she showed up at one of her old haunts."

The front door opened and all three men jumped to their feet.

"Hey, did you see the Toronto cop car—" Emerson froze as he spotted Sergeant Homer. "What's going on? Is it Anthony?" He shifted his gaze to Lester.

"Em? Look!" Eleanor came up behind him, baby Anthony still clutched to her breast.

"He's home!" Emerson turned and embraced them. "We've got the little tyke back," he said, his face beaming with unmistakable joy.

"Mr. Emerson Norman, I need to speak with you. Alone, please." Homer grabbed his coat from where he'd left it on the banister and escorted Emerson out onto the front porch.

Eleanor's eyes narrowed as she looked to Lester, who shrugged. "It'll be fine. Just routine," he said.

"The kettle's boiled if anyone would like some tea," she said.

"No, thank you," Mark said. "I am sure you want some time alone with your family. As soon as Sergeant Homer is finished speaking with Emerson, we'll all be out of your hair."

Charley followed Mark out to his car.

"I'll drive you back to the *Trib*."

"Thanks, but I want to go home. Now that baby Anthony's back, Lester can take over the story. The city is his beat." She got into the passenger seat, leaned back and closed her eyes in contemplation of a warm bath and a long sleep in her comfortable bed. She was glad that Anthony was safely home with his parents and especially relieved to learn that her article hadn't precipitated his abduction. But why hadn't Mark told her of his suspicions from the beginning?

It was on the tip of her tongue to ask him, but she stopped herself. What was the point? Either he'd tell her the truth and it would reveal another deep failing of her character or he'd feed her a lie in the mistaken belief he needed to soothe her hurt feelings. It didn't matter either way. The case was closed. She could go back to pretending he didn't exist.

"I'm sorry. I'm sorry. I'm coming."

Charley's indecision was going to make them late. She'd put her hair up, had taken it down and then put it up again. She tried on one outfit after another before finally settling on an elegant but modest burgundy-coloured gown with a high-neck collar and three-quarter length sleeves. As she took one last look in the mirror, she still wasn't entirely happy with the result.

What did one wear to the wedding of a former suitor/best friend?

The dog-whistle stopped her halfway down the stairs. "What are you doing here?"

"Well, merry Christmas to you, too, Tiger."

Mark grinned up at her, looking like the refined gentleman she knew he was not. Not only was he clean-shaven, but his hair was shorter and more fashionably cut than she'd seen it before. He wore a black suit and tie underneath his unbuttoned woolen overcoat.

"The detective is going to escort us to the wedding." Gran held up a book that was still partially encased in festive wrapping. "And look: he brought me a book. A signed first edition of *The Big Sleep*, by Raymond Chandler."

"To broaden your reading in the genre," Mark said, grinning. He held up a brass plate inscribed with his name and business. "And I thank you for your thoughtful gift, Bessie. I shall take great pleasure in attaching it to my office door. It will certainly raise my cachet and perhaps attract a better calibre of client." He winked at Charley and reached into his coat pocket.

"I didn't know we were exchanging gifts," Charley said quickly, fearful that he was about to present her with one. When she had finally gotten around to compiling the list of gifts she would give to her friends—the expensive tea Grace enjoyed and a colourful scarf for Laine—she had briefly considered buying something for Mark and just as quickly dismissed the idea. They were not friends. She hadn't seen him nor spoken to him since the end of November when he'd returned baby Anthony to his parents.

Mark's hand remained in his pocket. "We're not. I merely saw the book in a bookshop and thought your grandmother might enjoy it."

"Hurry up and get your coat, Charlotte," Gran said. "I don't want to be late."

"But I called Mr. Arcadi and arranged for him to drive us," Charley said.

"And I called him to cancel. There is no reason to take Mr. Arcadi away from his family on Christmas Eve."

Mark took Charley's coat from Rachel and held it out for her to slip into.

"I'm a little surprised you were invited," she said, stepping away from him as quickly as she could.

"I'm family."

"When it suits you."

He chuckled and held open the door. "After you, ladies."

THE BALLROOM OF THE BANKSES' mansion glittered with bright silver lights. The chairs and tables were covered with a merry red fabric in keeping with the season.

Meredith wore a simple white satin gown and was escorted up the aisle by her brother, who remained by her side at the altar. *That is odd*, Charley thought. The woman had been here for two years and yet she had no female friend to stand up with her?

Dan, looking dapper in a dark tuxedo, waited for his bride alongside his father, who was serving as his best man. That struck her as strange, too. Dan had always been popular, and she knew he had a tonne of friends from both his university and rowing days as well as from his work at the city.

In sharp contrast to the tiny and insular wedding party, the guest list consisted of more than one hundred members of Kingston's social, political, and business elite.

Charley kept her eyes focused on the minister and forced her face into a mask of polite indifference. She could feel Mark's sharp gaze on her throughout the ceremony. Gran was as bad, taking her hand and squeezing it sympathetically. What did they think she was going to do? Stand up and protest when the minister asked if anyone objected to the union? She'd come to terms with Dan's decision to marry Meredith some time ago.

But as the minister introduced the couple as husband and wife, she felt the air ripped from her lungs and she emitted a small gasp. Fortunately, the resounding applause covered the sound, although Mark and Gran both noticed. She pasted a smile on her face and began to clap her hands enthusiastically along with everyone else.

Once the formalities were over, the chairs were pushed back, clearing the way for a dance floor. Charley walked over to the dessert table. She wasn't hungry, but she also wasn't keen to watch the various members of the wedding party take their turn on the dance floor.

Mark followed her along, piling his plate with colourful pastries.

"As 'family' shouldn't you be dancing," she said irritably.

He glanced over and shrugged. "I think they've got it covered."

"You don't have to babysit me, you know. I'm fine."

"I know." He popped a *macaron* into his mouth. "Are you going to eat that?" He pointed at the cherry tart she'd put on her plate and added it to his own when she shook her head. "You're better off without him, Tiger. You know that, right?"

"You have made your opinion clear." She turned and walked away from him.

"Ah, Mrs. Hall," Colin Banks intercepted her. "I was hoping to have the opportunity to speak with you tonight." He took her arm and led her to an alcove between two of the floor-to-ceiling windows that lined one side of the room.

"It was a lovely ceremony," Charley said taking full advantage of Gran's social etiquette training.

"Yes, thank you. It meant a lot to Meredith and Dan that you came."

"Dan and I have been good friends since childhood, and the few times I've met Meredith...well, she's quite lovely."

"I understand she told you the details of our past." He'd lowered his voice. "I trust you will keep it to yourself."

"I told her I would."

His eyes narrowed. "She is very trusting. I am afraid, I am not so much."

"Is my word not good enough for you?"

"You are a reporter. It's your job to ferret out scandal."

"I don't make things up, though. If what your sister told me is the truth, you have nothing to fear from me."

"And if you uncover some inconsistencies?"

Inconsistencies wouldn't be uncommon. She knew from interviewing many people about the same event that they often saw and interpreted things differently. She had the impression, however, that Banks was hinting at something more significant. "What are you asking?"

"I simply want to know how far your loyalty to our good friend Dan Cannon extends?"

"And by extension to you?"

"Charley, there you are!" Dan broke into their conversation. "I was hoping to have a dance. You don't mind if I take her away, do you, Colin?"

Banks' face flushed slightly. Charley had a distinct impression he had more to say and he minded very much that Dan wanted to take her away. But he waved his hand, dismissing them. "Not at all, old chap. This is your day."

She followed Dan onto the dance floor, glad to be away from Colin Banks and his dulcet-toned voice that may or may not have been issuing a threat. Dan was part of his family now. What *would* she do if she found out Banks was tied up in something sinister? The police hadn't been able to connect him to Bigelow or Carruthers, but that didn't mean he wasn't involved with the gambling syndicate, only that there was no hard evidence of it.

Banks' question wouldn't leave her: How far did her loyalty to Dan extend?

"It was a lovely ceremony," Charley murmured again in

the span of a few minutes as Dan wrapped his arm around her waist and led her in a bouncy waltz.

"Ouch." He grinned down at her. "So proper, Mrs. Hall. What happened to my friend, Charley?"

She swatted him with her free hand and then returned it to his shoulder. They moved easily together, their long history giving them the ability to anticipate the other's intention by the subtlest of body movements. The music slowed and she leaned in closer and rested her cheek against his shoulder. She hadn't given the act any forethought; it was what she'd always done. But he stiffened and she straightened up right away. "Sorry, old habit," she said, feeling both disappointment and embarrassment in equal parts.

"Can I cut in?" Mark asked.

She tried not to be offended by how quickly Dan dropped his hands and stepped back. She remembered a time, not too long ago—in this very home, in fact—when they'd almost come to blows over her.

Although his style was more controlling than Dan's, Mark was an exceptionally good dancer.

"Don't be so surprised," Mark chided her when she commented on it. "The nuns were quite insistent we learn the social graces."

"You must pick and choose which ones you decide to follow."

He chuckled. "Like my attachment to the Cannon family, I acknowledge them when it suits."

"How does coming to Dan's wedding suit you?"

"I would think that would be obvious, Tiger. It allows me to see you. Barring another murder, you have made it quite clear you want nothing to do with me."

"Can you blame me?"

"Not at all. But someday you'll have to acknowledge I was right about your feelings—or should I say lack of feelings—for my half-brother, and I intend to be around for that."

"To say 'I told you so'?"

"Among other things." He executed a perfect *chassé*, but she was unprepared for the triple step and stumbled. "Careful, Tiger. You'll have to pay attention if you're going to keep up."

Among other things.

It was after midnight when they arrived back home. During the drive, Mark's comment kept coming back like an itch she couldn't quite reach to scratch.

Mark walked them to the door. Rachel had already retired for the night, so he helped the women remove their coats. Gran thanked him, wished him a merry Christmas and excused herself to go directly up to bed.

Among other things.

What other things?

Perhaps the package she'd caught a glimpse of earlier? Despite her resolve to ignore it, she couldn't help wondering what he had brought for her? And why?

"If you keep staring at my pocket like that, you're going to burn a hole right through my coat," Mark said.

"You're being ridiculous."

"Am I?" One eyebrow raised quizzically, and his hand hovered over his pocket.

"Oh, all right." Darn him anyway! "Yes, I am curious."

"You know what they say about curiosity and cats, don't you, Tiger?" He retrieved the present and twirled it between his fingers.

It was a slightly larger than his palm, square and wrapped in shiny silver paper with a red ribbon.

"I don't have a Christmas present for you," Charley said.

Mark frowned. "I didn't get this for you because I expected something in return. I saw it in a shop and thought you might like it. But if it makes you feel better, your birthday's next week, right?" He handed her the package. "Happy birthday."

She tugged on the ribbon and carefully removed the wrapping paper, revealing a plain white box. She lifted the lid and gasped.

"Do you like it?" Mark asked.

She ran her fingers gently over the intricately carved ivory hair comb. It was about four-inches square with a row of five tiny pansies topped by an elegant tiara design. "It's beautiful."

Mark picked up the comb and told her to turn around. "You're always fussing with your hair, putting it up or taking it down, tucking it this way and that." He inserted the comb into her chignon.

As she reached up to touch the comb, her fingers brushed his. She dropped her hand quickly and tried to gather her wits. It was a thoughtful gift, revealing, once again, his knack for observation and keen insight into another's personality. "Thank you."

"Frankly, I like it better when you leave your hair loose," he said close to her ear. "But I guess that's not the fashion among the social elite."

And, of course, he had to spoil the moment with another of his critical assessments of her.

She turned to face him, taking a step back. He was far too close. "Be careful, Detective. With your new family, you're becoming part of the very social elite you like to disparage. And speaking of the Cannons, are you spending tomorrow—or should I say, today—with them?"

"Perish the thought!" Mark shuddered. "No, fortunately when Rose got around to asking me to join them, I already had plans for the day."

"Oh?"

"Disappointed? Were you about to invite me to revel with you here? You'll have to be faster off the mark. I'm a popular guy."

Until this moment she hadn't thought of it. Frankly, she was a bit surprised Gran hadn't done so. The two seemed to be getting pretty cozy.

"I can see you're concerned, Tiger, so let me put your mind at ease. I have been invited to enjoy some punch with Miss Fletcher and Dr. Black—to celebrate the doc's home-coming—and then I am going to dine with Constable Marillo and his family. His wife, by the way, is an excellent cook. Now, I should be off." He executed a deep, mocking bow.

"Merry Christmas, Mark."

"Happy birthday, Charley."

∘——— ———∘

SHE WAS ON EDGE. Why did she allow Mark and his opinions get to her? The man confounded her. His gift was lovely. Why couldn't he have left it at that? But instead, he'd had to add a subtle censure.

Charley wandered into the drawing room. Perhaps a small sherry would settle her nerves and allow her to her fall asleep.

The Christmas tree they'd decorated as a family earlier

in the week twinkled brightly as the light of the room's lamps reflected off the metallic stars on the boughs. That had been a lovely afternoon. Everyone—and by that she meant Evelyn—had behaved themselves. Her maternal grandmother had seemed genuinely interested in hearing about their childhood Christmases—even Charley's memories. Gran, as magnanimous as ever, had encouraged Evelyn to reminisce about her daughter and Charley lapped up the new information, her mother transitioning from a notion to an actual living person.

The tree shimmied.

"Freddie! Aren't you a little old to be snooping for presents?"

Her brother backed out from under the tree, stood and turned to face her, a sheepish grin on his face. "I was checking."

"Are you afraid I forgot you?"

"No, but I was curious to see whether you got a present for Grandmama. I'm glad you did."

Charley nodded and collapsed into her chair. "It would be awkward if I didn't, don't you think?"

"I know her being here has been difficult for you." He sat down on the couch across from her. "I'm curious though: what did you get her?"

"Don't you want to wait and be surprised tomorrow morning?"

He shrugged.

"I asked Grace to help me create a scrapbook of articles about our mother. Not only the tributes after she died— although they're in there—but all of her charitable and community work. She was here for only six years, but she contributed so much in that short time."

"That's a perfect gift," Freddie said.

"I know Evelyn regrets her estrangement from her daughter. I thought knowing that she'd made a good life for herself here would give her some comfort."

"How was the wedding?" Freddie asked, suddenly changing the subject.

"Fine." She stood, restless again, and walked to the window. Flakes of snow had started to fall. They were the first of the season and perfectly timed for Christmas morning. She turned back to her brother. "What have you been doing all evening—aside from checking to see if Santa brought you any gifts."

Freddie cocked his head and for a moment she thought he was going to challenge her deflection, but instead he said, "After I brought Grandmama home from the church service, I went to see Laine and Grace to wish them an early merry Christmas. I haven't been home very long myself."

Charley had helped Grace move Laine home the previous day. Her friend hoped to resume her medical studies after New Year's, although in a limited manner. Laine had confided to her that she was nervous, but Charley was certain that with the support of everyone at the hospital —and Grace—she would be successful.

"Not so early now. It's Christmas morning," Charley said. "Merry Christmas, Freddie."

"Merry Christmas, Charley." His smile disappeared and he stroked his beard thoughtfully. "There's something I've been meaning to talk to you about."

"You sound so serious." She knew something had been on Freddie's mind since he'd mentioned the need to make restitution when they'd been at the hospital with Laine last month. "Maybe it should wait. Christmas isn't the time—"

"It can't wait anymore. I *need* to do this."

Restitution for harm done. That's what the program

required. But was she strong enough to hear what he had to tell her? She sat down on the couch and looked into her brother's troubled eyes. If he needed this to ensure his sobriety, could she deny him? "Okay."

"It's about Theo."

Of course it was about Theo. She closed her eyes and pictured the young man she'd married in order for him to have someone to come home to after the war. A man she'd been faithful to, at least physically. She'd never been in love with him—at least not like a wife should love her husband—but she had loved him. And she'd honoured her promise to wait for his return even when everyone else told her to give up and move on with her life.

"You do know he's dead, right?"

Her brother's words ripped at the threads she'd so tightly stitched around her identity as the persevering wife.

Freddie didn't wait for her to reply. "I know we haven't spoken about him since I returned. We liked to pretend." His voice wavered. "But the truth of it was too awful to—"

"How? When?" Why was she asking? It would make it real. Once and for all, finally real.

"On the beach at Dieppe. As soon as we came ashore. He died in my arms."

Dieppe.

Six years ago.

She'd been a widow for six years.

No, six seconds. Until six seconds ago, she was still a wife—a wife whose husband was simply missing. Missing but not dead.

Theo is dead.

Oh, the poor, dear boy. Was he afraid? Had he suffered? The images she'd seen...the stories she'd heard... At least Freddie had been with him. His best friend. Perhaps that had provided Theo some comfort in the end. But the cost to her brother...

"Charley?" Freddie knelt in front of her. "Tell me you knew. You had to have known. It's been so long."

She reached out and cupped his cheek, the soft bristles of his red beard tickled her palm.

Was it possible to know but not know?

Mark had accused her of deliberately denying it because she didn't love Dan enough to marry him—didn't want to marry another man she wasn't in love with. But that wasn't entirely true. Freddie had returned home after they'd thought he'd been killed at Dieppe. Was it so hard to imagine that Theo could do the same?

And yet, when she examined her heart, she was forced to realize that after all this time, Theo had become more a part of who *she* was rather than an actual separate person. If he was gone, who was Charley Hall?

Her brother stared up at her. His eyes pleading with her to understand.

Poor Freddie. He'd suffered more than anyone. He and Theo had been thick as thieves since their mothers had met as war brides, carrying infant sons on the ship from England. They even shared the same birth date. Freddie had been there, had held Theo while he died. It is no wonder he'd turned to alcohol after he returned from the war. It wasn't the German POW camp he was trying to forget, it was the memories of his best friend that were everywhere.

"Yes, I knew." She'd intended to cross her fingers behind her back but realized she couldn't. There were many layers to knowing.

Maybe some day she'd ask Freddie to tell her more about how it had happened. But not today. It had taken everything within her brother to give her this much. And it had taken everything within herself to let him be at peace with it. For now, it was enough.

She was still sitting in her chair, staring out the window and watching the snow fall, when Rachel entered the drawing room hours later to start the fire and begin the early morning baking.

"Would you like me to bring you a cup of coffee?"

"No, thank you." Charley stood and stretched. "I think I'll get a few hours of sleep before the festivities begin. Merry Christmas, Rachel."

"Merry Christmas, Mrs. Hall."

In a week Charley would turn thirty—on January 1st. But the Charley Hall that would begin a new decade of her life wasn't the same woman she'd been at the start of 1948. It wasn't about what she'd lost—her job, Dan, Theo—but about what she'd gained, too. She had a loving family, good friends, and a purpose to her life. Oh sure, there was a lot she could improve upon—Mark could always be counted on to point out her flaws—but overall, she liked who she'd become.

Was becoming.

Because she wasn't done yet.

Want more? How about an art heist that gets a little too personal for our feisty reporter?

Chasing a band of murderous art thieves brings Charley face-to-face with a past she'd rather forget.

Get *Murder in Abstract* to see the whole picture today! And keep reading for a sneak peek.

Want more from Charley and her friends? Head over to my website and sign up for the *Gayle Gazette* to keep up-to-date on new releases, exclusive access to special features and giveaways. Plus, you'll get a free download of a solve-it-yourself *Bessie Stormont Whodunit*. Yup, Gran has some real detective skills, too.

Is this your first Charley Hall Mystery? Get *A Shot of Murder,* book 1 in the series, and follow Charley and the gang from the beginning.

If you enjoyed *Odds on Murder*, please consider leaving a review at your favourite e-retailer or GoodReads so other readers can discover the Charley Hall historical mystery series.

HISTORICAL NOTES

Generally, when I write the Charley Hall mysteries, I like to spend some time in the national archives researching local newspaper articles from the period covered in the book to get interesting tidbits that can enhance the story. Unfortunately, the planning and writing of *Odds on Murder* was done while we were all self-isolating to stop the spread of COVID-19, so instead, I turned to the Internet, which doesn't have the same wealth of interesting local trivia. However, in addition to the weather data, which I try to make as accurate as possible, there are a few stories of note that informed the writing of this book.

THE ABDUCTION OF BABY ANTHONY

Much of the story surrounding the abduction of Anthony Pyne is based on a true story and comes from an article I'd previously "clipped" when researching *A Diagnosis of Murder* (Book 3). On page 11, the *Kingston Whig-Standard* (August 11, 1948) reported on the arrest of a young woman who had abducted the infant son of her lover in retaliation for his refusal to marry her. The woman, who did have a criminal record and had spent time at the Mercer Reformatory for theft, took particularly good care of the baby and was perceived to be genuinely attached to it. The father didn't want to press charges stating: "She comes from a good home and I think it was the lure of big cars and cocktail bars that led her astray."

PROVINCIAL INQUIRY INTO ORGANISED GAMBLING

In one of those purely serendipitous Google searches, I came across a report examining organized gambling in the province of Ontario.

"My investigation disclosed that commencing about the forties there was an alarming upsurge in organized gambling in this province particularly in gaming. It was carried on in premises ostensibly occupied and operated by incorporated social clubs but the real operators were professional gamblers." (*Report of The Honourable Mr. Justice Wilfrid D. Roach as a Commissioner Appointed Under the Public Inquiries Act by Letters Patent, December 11, 1961, p. 12*)

Over 400 pages long, the commissioner's report details how these gaming houses were set up and operated. It also includes accounts by members of the Ontario Provincial Police's Anti-Gambling Branch of the syndicates' attempts to recruit police officers. The statements Charley reads in Chapter 23 are almost verbatim descriptions from the report—with names and key details changed, of course.

KINGSTON'S ANNEXATION OF KINGSTON TOWNSHIP

The annexation moving the municipal boundary of the City of Kingston to the west side of the mouth of the Little Cataraqui River at Cataraqui Bay on the north shore of Lake Ontario took place in 1952. After World War II, the land west of the city, in Kingston Township, saw considerable commercial development but it did not become part of the City of Kingston until amalgamation in 1998. If you'd like to know more about Kingston's various annexations, I will refer you to Frances Mary Willis's *A study to examine the boundary expansions of Kingston from a legal and land perspective, with emphasis on the 1998 amalgamation* (A thesis submitted to the School of Urban and Regional Planning, Queen's University, in accordance with the requirements for the Degree of Master of Urban and Regional Planning, 2014).

SNEAK PEEK: MURDER IN ABSTRACT

A CHARLEY HALL MYSTERY, BOOK 5

CHARLEY TRAILED Mark to the foyer. "So, what's next?"

"What I'd really like is to see Mrs. Overstreet's art studio. The police were in and out—Marillo said there was nothing there—but now it's locked up tight. The senator says it's because his wife doesn't allow anyone in her studio, not even the housekeeper. So, until we can speak to her..." He left the rest of the sentence hanging.

"What do you think you'll find in the studio?"

"I don't know. I'm trying to figure out why someone would want to steal a collection of paintings done by a woman who hasn't even had her first formal art show. What's so special about them? Or was it something else they were after?"

"Follow me." Charley made an abrupt turn and led Mark toward the east wing.

"Hey, hold up, Tiger." Mark grabbed her arm. "Don't you think I already tried to get in?"

"Oh, ye of little faith." Charley wrenched her arm away and continued to the wing's entrance. She tried to turn the doorknob, but it wouldn't budge.

"See? I told you so."

She cocked an eyebrow at his smugness. Mark Spadina had a habit of getting the better of her, but not this time. She stood on her toes and reached up to the top of the door jamb.

Please, be here.

She ran her fingertips along the smooth surface, her heart racing. It would be so embarrassing to be wrong.

No, wait. There it is!

She plucked the key from its resting place and slid it into the lock, swinging the door open with a flourish. "You were saying?"

"I'm impressed," Mark said, following her into the room. "What other Overstreets secrets do you know?"

"You'll have to wait and see."

The entire wing appeared to be one huge room, brightly lit from the large windows along the front and back exterior walls. It was a perfect art studio, just as it had been a perfect rumpus room when she'd played here in her youth. Gone were the shelves of games and books, and the grand dollhouse she'd envied. In their place was...nothing. No easels, no canvases, no paint, no brushes. The only telltale sign that anyone had been in here recently was the melted slush from the boots of whoever had taken the paintings and the police officers who'd come to investigate the theft.

"I'm guessing that despite the senator's claim that no one is allowed in the wing, the housekeeper comes in to clean. That's how you knew where the key was?" Mark said, scanning the room.

"Maybe. But when I was last here, the room was considered off-limits, too—it was supposed to be for the children, no adults allowed. Mrs. Rinehart kept a key hidden, of course, so she could check on the room, but it was up to us to keep it neat and tidy." Charley swung her arm around dramatically. "But this?" She couldn't imagine, given the aggressive, almost violent application of paint she'd seen in the artwork last evening that there'd be no trace of it in the studio. The woman who'd created those paintings didn't seem to be the sort who would be fanatical about keeping her art studio pristine. "Even if Mrs. Rinehart was coming in to tidy, why is there no splash of paint anywhere?"

"There's not much of anything," Mark agreed. "But you know how temperamental these creative types can be. Maybe she was taking a break or suffering from whatever the painter's equivalent is for writer's block," Mark said, coming to stand beside her. "Speaking of temperamental creatives, do you want to let me in on your history with the Overstreet family?"

"Not really."

Mark crossed his arms and pierced her with one of his penetrating stares.

"It was a long time ago. Until last night, I hadn't been here in years." She squirmed under his scrutiny. "Besides, it has nothing to do with the case."

"Hmm. There didn't seem to be any tension between you and the senator," Mark mused. "And Mrs. Rinehart seemed genuinely pleased to see you. Mrs. Overstreet?"

"You're fishing, Detective. And wasting our time."

"Finding more out about you is never a waste of my time, Tiger," Mark teased. "Let's see, now, if it's not Mrs. Over—"

"Well, well, well, look who the cat dragged in!"

Charley stiffened. *Great!* Slowly, she turned around to face the inevitable.

Mark stepped past her. "You must be Poppy. We were just talking about you."

Want to read more?
Get *Murder in Abstract,* book 5 in the Charley Hall Mystery series.

ACKNOWLEDGEMENTS

Writing is a solitary pursuit but publishing a book is not. I am forever grateful to two talented author/editors who are instrumental in bringing my stories to you.

Joanna D'Angelo, my friend and editor, who suggested I write a mystery series and brainstormed ideas with me during a long drive to Toronto and back—and then hounded me until I actually wrote it.

Carolyn Heald, a historian, archivist and talented writer in her own right, she is also—and truly fortunate for me—an excellent copy editor who is very familiar with the city of Kingston as well as proper grammar.

In addition, over the past year I have been supported by the great team at Best Page Forward, who have taught me so much about the self-publishing world.

Finally, I want to express my sincere appreciation to the members of the Ottawa Romance Writers, the Women's Fiction Writers Association, Crime Writers of Canada, and Sisters in Crime, who provide unconditional support and a safe space to ask questions in this strange world of fiction writing.

ABOUT BRENDA GAYLE

I've been a writer all my life but returned to my love of fiction after more than 20 years in the world of corporate communications—although some might argue there is plenty of opportunity for fiction-writing there, too. I have a Master's degree in journalism and an undergraduate degree in psychology. A fan of many genres, I find it hard to stay within the publishing industry's prescribed boxes. Whether it's historical mystery, romantic suspense, or women's fiction, my greatest joy is creating deeply emotional books with memorable characters and compelling stories.

Connect with me on my website at BrendaGayle.com & sign up for *The Gayle Gazette,* my newsletter, to keep up-to-date on new releases, exclusive access to special features, giveaways, and all sorts of shenanigans. And don't forget, as a subscriber, you'll get a free download of a *Bessie Stormont Whodunit.*

Until next time...

ALSO BY BRENDA GAYLE

CHARLEY HALL MYSTERY SERIES

A Shot of Murder

Rigged for Murder

A Diagnosis of Murder

Odds on Murder

Murder in Abstract

Schooled in Murder